THE BRIDE'S FIRST HOME BOOK

Ruth Rejnis has had ten years' experience on the real estate news staff of *The New York Times* and is now a contributing editor of *Savvy*. She is the author of *All America's Real Estate* (with Carolyn Janik), which is available from Penguin, and five other books on real estate and housing. She lives in Hoboken, New Jersey.

ALSO BY RUTH REJNIS

All America's Real Estate Book (with Carolyn Janik)
The Single Parent's Housing Guide
Her Home: A Woman's Guide to Buying Real Estate
How to Buy Real Estate Without Getting Burned
A Woman's Guide to New Careers in Real Estate
Everything Tenants Need to Know to Get Their Money's Worth

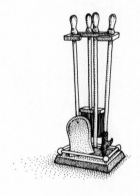

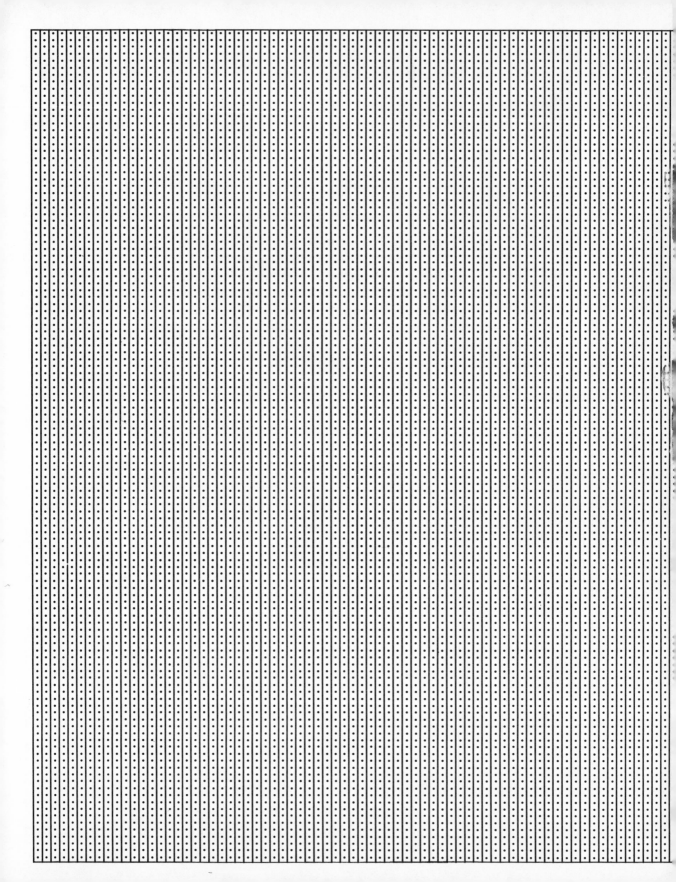

T·H·E
BRIDE'S
FIRST
HOME
BOOK

Finding and Creating a Special Place
for the Two of You

R·U·T·H R·E·J·N·I·S

ILLUSTRATIONS BY BOB JOHNSON

PENGUIN BOOKS

PENGUIN BOOKS
Published by the Penguin Group
Viking Penguin, a division of Penguin Books USA Inc.,
40 West 23rd Street, New York, New York 10010, U.S.A.
Penguin Books Ltd, 27 Wrights Lane,
London W8 5TZ, England
Penguin Books Australia Ltd, Ringwood,
Victoria, Australia
Penguin Books Canada Ltd, 2801 John Street,
Markham, Ontario, Canada L3R 1B4
Penguin Books (N.Z.) Ltd, 182–190 Wairau Road,
Auckland 10, New Zealand

Penguin Books Ltd, Registered Offices:
Harmondsworth, Middlesex, England

First published in Penguin Books 1989
Published simultaneously in Canada

1 3 5 7 9 10 8 6 4 2

Copyright © Ruth Rejnis, 1989
Illustrations copyright © Viking Penguin, a division of
Penguin Books USA Inc., 1989
All rights reserved

Library of Congress Cataloging in Publication Data
Rejnis, Ruth.
The bride's first home book: finding and creating a special place
for the two of you / Ruth Rejnis.
p.   cm.
ISBN 0 14 01.1404 1
1. House buying.   2. Home economics.   3. Sexual division of labor.
I. Title.   II. Title: Bride's 1st home book.
HD1379.R449   1989
643′.12—dc19   88-29410

Printed in the United States of America
Set in Cheltenham Light
Designed by Joel Avirom

For every bride
With wishes for much luck and happiness
as you create this new home

C O N T E N T S

T·H·E
BRIDE'S
FIRST
HOME
BOOK

NEW BEGINNINGS

Your wedding, the start of a new life, the setting up of a new home. These are happy and busy days for you, with probably a few nail-biting ones now and then, too.

This book is here to help. It is directed at you as a bride, but its words are in many instances meant for your husband as well. He may have deferred to you in wedding preparations, but his voice will certainly be heard, and his opinion obviously valued, in your search for an apartment, in considering whether you can afford to buy a house, in "animated discussions" about who does which part of the housework. He will be as interested as you are in most of these household, and househunting, matters, and likely to be just as much at sea as you are about others.

Listen to Todd, who married Christine, and even at the somewhat ripe age of twenty-eight was bemused initially at the turnaround in his life:

"I didn't understand the role of a wedding in society, and why we had to go through all that hoopla. There's a symbolism in all of this, someone told me. Christine and I have gone through a rite of passage, not just legally, but in human and cultural terms, too. Now I see how it all fits in. Weddings and wedding gifts are society's way of acknowledging the presence of a new household, its way of helping a couple start a home."

That home can be a farmhouse on a hundred acres of land, a few rooms in campus housing or on a military base, a suburban Tudor, or a three-and-a-half-room apartment in a 250-unit condominium community.

Your first home is probably far from what you hope to live in someday. But if you cannot start with a formal dining room, and if the bedroom is too small for the canopy bed you have dreamed of, and the yard you wanted is missing, and in fact there is not a tree in sight, you can still create a charming, attractive place in which to live with the possessions you do have and will acquire in these early days. With love, humor, and generosity of spirit, you will be creating memories to be cherished in this first home, no matter what it is lacking. They will be memories you will carry with you as you rent or buy other apartments, condos, or houses together. In time, this first year at home as husband and wife will be part of the haze of what will become your family history—a haze that can be very golden. The noisy air-conditioner, the eccentric next-door neighbor, the stashed-away wedding gifts that never did fit in, the too-crowded apartment—you wouldn't have missed them for the world!

The facts and advice in *The Bride's First Home Book*—about mortgages, moving companies, decorators, and insurance—will steer you toward wise housing and investment decisions as your finances, careers, and even attitudes toward your next home evolve. There is something missing in these pages, however, that cannot be furnished by an outsider. Since the concept of "home" began—and things are no different today—it has been the bride, now the wife, who has supplied that intangible quality that makes the simplest or grandest dwelling a home. Your contribution rounds out the picture. While the words on these pages will help you with a house, *you* will create a home.

1

WHEN IT MAKES SENSE TO RENT YOUR HOME

Y ou will probably start married life as a tenant. You may move on to another place in a year or two or three, renting again. Perhaps it bothers you that you will not be buying a house now, or maybe renting is your choice. Even if you feel you should be buying, there is good news: you may be wise to remain in that apartment for the next several years.

Let's take a look at six couples, three newly married, three married for more than a year (which takes the women past the "bride" stage), who live in the same metropolitan area in the East. They are all tenants, for various reasons.

Dani and Steve (you'll learn more about them in Chapter 2) are newlyweds who moved into an apartment. But the day they can afford a downpayment and closing costs on a condominium, and feel they can carry a monthly mortgage payment, they will be off to see a real estate agent. They are not sure when that will be and concede that they often worry that the price of houses will be rising faster than their savings balance.

Laura and Mike have been married three years. After their wedding, Laura moved into Mike's rather spacious rent-controlled apartment. No doubt, their landlord is not happy about the rent ceiling, but Laura and Mike are delighted that they are paying, they calculate, about $200 less than prevailing rents for an apartment of that size in that city. The savings have enabled them to purchase an inexpensive country home, a few counties away, for weekend use. That house, Laura and Mike expect, will be their only real estate investment for a while. They do not intend to give up their apartment.

Rebeka and Paul have been renting for three years. Rebeka is employed; Paul is completing his dissertation for a Ph.D. in economics. They cannot afford to buy a home until Paul earns his degree and they become a two-income couple.

Tina and Ernie have been married for just six months but have no plans at all to buy their own home. A year ago Ernie bought a coffee shop from the owner, who was retiring. Most of the couple's money is being used to pay off that loan; any amount left over is plowed back into the business. Ernie, whose background is Hispanic, plans to turn the coffee shop into an inexpensive Mexican restaurant eventually. Tina works full-time as a word processor. It will be several years before the couple

feel free financially to buy a house—unless, they point out, they hit it *very* big with the coffee shop–restaurant. They are already thinking of opening chains in their area.

Sunny and Tom can afford to buy. They have been married four years, and both hold good-paying jobs. But for the last year or so, Tom has not been happy with his career. The changes at the office that were promised him have not materialized. He is at the point now of considering whether to stay with that firm or move on to something new. Perhaps, if he decides to switch jobs, the couple will move to another part of the country. Both agree this is no time for homebuying.

Shelley and Art have been married just under a year. They rent a city apartment they love, and have no desire to own a home. They are not interested in home maintenance or gardening, and they do not plan to have children. They thought about purchasing a cooperative or condominium, logical options for those who prefer low-maintenance homeowning, but even that proved too much of a commitment for them. They just plain prefer to rent.

All of these folks' reasons for renting are valid. Homeowning is not for everyone, and for some, not right at certain stages of their lives. Two of these couples, however, should be a little concerned about their housing picture. More about them later.

The Wisdom of Renting

Something happened a few years before your wedding. The real estate boom of the last decade leveled off a bit. For a while, househunters were able to capitalize on low home prices and low interest rates. Everyone wanted to get into homeownership before prices or interest rates rose again—which, since real estate is cyclical, they were bound to do.

Those days of flurry and quick turnover abated eventually, however. Today, unless you live in a "hot" city or region of the country, where housing costs are still rising more than the national average, you have little prospect of building equity quickly in a home. ("Equity" is a term you will hear often once you get involved in homebuying. It refers to the value an owner has in a piece of property, exclusive of its mortgage and any other liens. For instance, if the market value of a house is $100,000, and the owner has paid off $7,000 of a $75,000 mortgage, leaving $68,000, the owner has $32,000 equity.)

So buying a home as a rapidly appreciating investment does not offer the lure it once did. Homes are bought today as places in which to live, with the hope that the investment will pay off one day when the owner sells. That payoff is not likely to happen very soon after purchase, however. It costs money to get into homeownership nowadays, and, all things being equal, one must stay in a particular house at least two or three years to make a profit.

A home is an illiquid investment, too. You cannot quickly get at the money you have invested if you need it for an emergency.

It must be said, however, that over the long haul, buying a home is the wiser course for most Americans to pursue—for investment purposes, pride of ownership, and emotional security. For the short term, though—and that may mean years—renting may well be the better solution, given certain personal and financial situations.

For what types of tenants might renting be a sensible decision?

- Childless couples. Buying a home comes about frequently with the birth of the first, or certainly the second, child. Until then, many couples feel they can continue with the relatively carefree tenant life.

- Frequent transferees. Settlement costs and moving expenses make it hard not to lose money when buying and selling houses quickly in these situations.

- Those who live in an area with inexpensive, plentiful rental housing. Some sections of the country have become overbuilt, especially with condominiums, in recent years. The result is that rents there are at irresistible, rock-bottom levels.

- Renters who do not feel comfortable buying at the moment because of circumstances having nothing to do with housing affordability. *You* might fit into this category. You have just been married, and may feel that marriage is a large enough change in your lives for the moment. You may prefer to wait a while before buying.

- Tenants who have no time for, and no interest in, home maintenance.

- Tumbling tumbleweeds, seemingly born footloose and fancy free, who are never in one place long enough even to consider the purchase of a house.

Who Is Missing Here?

The six couples mentioned earlier either have chosen renting as their permanent housing style or feel that renting is right for them at this time of their lives. But many couples feel trapped in apartment living. They want their own home and are frustrated and angry because they are unable to buy. They just cannot afford a house or condominium. The same scenario is acted out in apartment buildings around the nation: renters sitting over financial scribblings and wondering why they seem to be excluded from the homebuying market. What have they been doing wrong? they wonder. Dani and Steve have just begun saving for a condo; frustration hasn't entered the picture yet. But if the couple keep saving, and prices keep rising, and a home seems more and more beyond their grasp, the bitterness *will* set in.

Buying that first home *is* becoming increasingly difficult.

Many factors seem to have conspired to keep would-be first-timers from owning homes. The rising price of houses in many parts of the country is one factor. If you are unfortunate enough to be thinking of househunting one day in an extremely high-priced area (and such areas can vary from one year to the next), it is going to be even more difficult to become a homeowner.

Also, more mortgage lenders are demanding down payments of 15 to 20 percent on homes these days, as opposed to the relatively affordable 10 percent, or even less, of some years ago. Buyers today need a larger chunk of money, plus another sizable sum for closing costs (there is more information about both these expenses in later chapters). And nationally, the average monthly mortgage payment is now over $1,000.

Your response to those grim statistics may be to rent, if that monthly charge is substantially lower than the mortgage payment for a home in your part of the country. Or you may want to do

COMPUTER CLOSE-UP

For nearly a decade Cornell University has offered renters a program titled "Buy or Rent? A Customized Housing Costs and Benefits Analysis." For more personalized information on what for some tenants is truly a dilemma, contact Buy-Rent Analysis, Consumer Economics and Housing Department, MVR Hall, Cornell University, Ithaca, N.Y. 14853, or call (607) 255-2587. They will send you a comprehensive questionnaire, to be returned to that office, that will focus on your own finances. The cost is $25 for two computer analyses, each slightly different in focus.

some investigating. Perhaps you can become homeowners by looking into housing styles you may never have considered, or by asking questions of mortgage lenders and learning about financing programs of whose existence you were unaware. That is what Dani and Steve should have been doing, even as they moved into their new apartment and began saving pennies and dollars for a home. (More information about possible solutions to buying when you think you don't have enough money will be found in upcoming chapters.)

Renting and Investing

The other couple who, if they are not already doing so, should be looking at their financial portfolio while they rent is Sunny and Tom, the two-career couple not at all interested in home-owning. If you rent, which means your savings are not going into equity buildup in a home, it is important for you to be saving money *somewhere*. Sunny and Tom may ultimately be driven to buy something by the need for tax deductions, which can be sizable with a house. Many renters start househunting after one disastrous April 15 too many. Mortgage interest and real estate taxes are deductible from your federal tax return, and these are the largest deductions most Americans have—and badly need.

If renting is cheap where you live, and you have no plans at the moment to buy, what you are saving with that low monthly payment should be invested, since your rent check does not bring you any saving or equity buildup. Are you both contributing at least 10 percent of your income every year to tax-deferred savings plans such as 401Ks to make up for that lack of mortgage interest deduction? Do you have stocks, bank savings certificates, or some other investments? Perhaps you have your eye on buying a home for occasional use rather than as a primary residence, as Laura and Mike have done. That purchase would bring *its* tax benefits, appreciation, and buildup in equity.

There is no foolproof way to compare renting with home-ownership and come up with the statement "We should rent" or "We would be better off owning." The economy shifts regularly from rosy to glum, and personal considerations also enter into the equation. Even *they* change as careers are reevaluated, fortunes rise and fall, and baby makes three.

If you don't want to buy, or if you can't buy at the moment, make the most of the years you will spend as a tenant, financially and otherwise. They may well be laying the groundwork for a solid housing future.

SHOULD YOU RENT, FOR THE TIME BEING?

	YES	NO
Do you plan to stay in your city, or area, for the next three or four years?		
Do you have enough money for a downpayment (15 to 20 percent of the purchase price) and closing costs (3 to 5 percent of the amount of the mortgage) on a home?		
Do you have the time for, and interest in, maintaining a home—mowing the lawn, fixing plumbing, etc.?		
Is there a scarcity of attractive, low-cost rental housing in your area?		
Are the prices of homes in your area increasing only at the rate of inflation, not skyrocketing beyond that figure?		
Do you have an established, solid credit record?		
As a two-career couple, are you being stung by income taxes?		
Can you afford to spend 30 to 35 percent of your income each month for housing costs (mortgage, real estate taxes, insurance)?		

If the majority of your answers fall in the "No" column, you are unquestionably better off renting, at least for now.

2

THE APARTMENT HUNT

Being organized people ("maybe a little too much so," Dani confides), Dani and Steve approached looking for an apartment in the same way they organized their wedding and set up a budget for the first couple of years of their marriage. Dani had been living with her parents, Steve in his own apartment. That was no decorator bachelor place, it was . . . a tad on the primitive side. There was no way the happy couple would start married life there, even the bridegroom conceded that. So the hunt began.

Dani and Steve's search is likely to be much like yours. Rental apartments may differ—architecturally and in rent, location, and other, finer points. But looking for a place to call home, and, in this instance, a first home, is a common experience. So Dani and Steve offer a look at that somewhat nerve-racking episode in their lives.

RENT: A FIRST CONSIDERATION

Wisely, Dani and Steve decided to stay within suggested guidelines and payment of no more than one-quarter of a month's joint income, although both were willing to stretch that a little for a building or complex that was truly posh. Since they lived in an area with a lively apartment market and moderate rents, they knew they could find what they wanted. In some areas of the country—New York City, for one, and some college towns—there is an extremely low vacancy rate and little choice but to pay top dollar for even the meanest flat—when you can find it. (You say that's what you're up against? See the "Hunting in a Tight Market" box, p. 28, for some guidance.)

If you decide you'd like to spend more for an apartment than perhaps you should, the building owner, more commonly called the landlord, may well shrug and let you go ahead. In home-buying, mortgage lenders hold very strictly to the belief that a certain percentage of your income, and no more, should go toward housing. You will have to present a list of your other long-term expenses, and they will be taken into account as the lender judges just how much more debt you can handle. Your mortgage will be for as much as X dollars, and that's it. But renting is different. The building owner, manager, or rental agent will ask about your income, and if it seems sufficient to pay the rent on that apartment, he or she is not likely to ask any more questions. Those individuals will not care that you may be planning to put out as much as 50 percent of your income each month on housing. So if the swimming pool and other niceties of upper-strata apartment communities appeal to you, be sure you know you may be paying for those amenities with many dinners of Chunky Soup. The landlord won't do that preliminary budgeting for you.

Don't be surprised to find a confusing array of rents being charged. Rent for an apartment in a private home may be more than in a flossy new high-rise tower. The tower rent may be lower than an older rental highrise just down the street (perhaps things are moving slowly in the newer building—it's an overbuilt market and the owner is knocking a few dollars off that monthly charge). Maybe a six-room house will rent for less than a three-room apartment in certain locations. And there lies the secret of the variety of figures you will come up against.

LOCATION

The three most important words in real estate, it is said, are "location," "location," and "location." You're reading them in this book for the first time here, and they will surface again in Chapter 12. In buying, this means that *where* a home is located usually determines its worth. The same is true in renting. You can probably tell from your present home where the high-priced apartment buildings are likely to be in your area, and where the more affordable neighborhoods can be found. What you are able to spend in rent will pretty much determine where you will conduct your search, although since you are not making the kind of investment you would with a home, you might decide on an only so-so neighborhood, where you might not want to *own* property but, for one reason or another, feel quite happy renting. So here rent comes first, then location.

Dani and Steve asked themselves the usual questions in narrowing down their choice: Which of the affordable areas is closest to work? Or would we rather be away from the madding crowd in town? If that's the case, how far can we go into suburban or country settings and still have a reasonable commute? Will that ride be just one train or bus, or does it require two fares? Will we have to buy a car, or perhaps even a second car? A quiet residential street may sound like bliss to a rattled inner-city inhabitant, but without a car how will simple chores like hauling groceries from the supermarket one and a half miles away be managed?

Dani and Steve both worked in the city in office skyscrapers, but both enjoyed walking and bicycling and had their eyes on a new health club in a nearby suburban enclave. They opted for that particular community, which was on a commuter rail line into town. There were several apartment buildings and complexes there, plus units in private homes, and they all ringed the small downtown business section, which ran for about six blocks through the heart of the community.

"We wanted to get out of the city," Dani recalls. "We would have preferred being farther out, even in the country, but by not living so far out on the train line we'll save a total of sixty dollars a month in commuting fares. That's nothing to sneeze at—for us, anyway. Steve has a car, and we expect to get by just using his. I don't want to spend the money for one, and I don't think we'll have to."

WHO IS OFFERING THE APARTMENT FOR RENT?

If you're looking in a private home, be sure to talk to the owner or someone with authority to lease to you. The person who offers a lease can vary from one building to the next. It may be the owner, the staff in his or her on-site office, a building management company in another part of town, or a local real estate agency. Building superintendents may offer lease applications you can fill out, but usually they must pass those applications on to an appropriate authority.

Finding a place in a larger complex may be complicated. Try contacting building management companies in your area to see which apartment houses they handle, whether there are vacancies, what the rental range is, and how to apply for a unit. Let's say you talk on the phone with John Brown at the ABC Management Company. You've noticed their nameplate on the front of Moderate Towers, a building that interests you.

He may tell you Moderate Towers has a few vacancies, but Charming Cove, which you've also inquired about, has a waiting list. If you'd like to come in and talk to anyone in the office, they'll offer you an application for Moderate Towers. They may put you on the waiting list for Charming Cove over the phone.

If you decide on the Towers and eventually become a tenant, you can call the management company when you have a question about the rent, or a complaint about maintenance, or an interest in subletting. These people handle the day-to-day business for the building owner. You pay them no fee. If the apartment in which you are interested is rented by the owner or his or her manager, with no outside real estate agent involved, you will not be charged a rental fee here either.

Finding an apartment through a real estate agent *does* mean a commission is involved. You will be charged one month's rent or a percentage of the annual rent. This, of course, is the most costly way to lease, since aside from the agent's fee, you will very likely have to pay one month's rent, plus a month's security deposit up front. It can come to a nice little bundle of change if you have to add an agent's commission. Still, if it's a cream puff of an apartment . . .

You should know that registering with real estate agents does not mean "Whew, now we can sit back and wait for them to call." You've still got to hustle; since they're maniacally busy, keep phoning and reminding these agents you're still interested and waiting to hear from them. If you call regularly, you may get that listing that just came in.

If you're shopping in an area with a very low vacancy rate, don't rely on real estate agents. You'll just be two of hundreds of applicants they have on file. It's too passive a way to apartment-hunt in a landlord's market.

Dani and Steven ran into a problem regarding who can offer an apartment for rent. Through a classified advertisement, they found a charming two-family home near the business center. They called, came around to the house, liked the apartment, and were, they thought, approved by the owner of the house, Mr. Bailey. That evening Steve had a phone call from Bailey. Sounding very apologetic, he withdrew his offer of the apartment. His wife and his mother-in-law, both of whom lived in the downstairs apartment with him, did not want a young couple. Young couples meant babies eventually, and neither woman wanted to be bothered with the noise and fuss *that* brought. He was sorry, he said, adding that he was sure the couple would find another place and wishing them well.

Was this discriminatory? Certainly seems to be. But owner-occupied homes of three units or less are not subject to *all* of the laws in force for multifamily dwellings. The couple certainly *could* successfully have brought charges against Bailey if the rejection had been on racial or religious grounds. Dani and Steve could have legally pursued even *their* turndown, but did not want the bother, and so they let it pass. Moral here? In a private-home situation, be sure you are approved by all whose okay is needed, and consult local housing laws so you know your legal rights if you want to take a stand.

Dani was so disturbed by this experience that the couple decided to confine their apartment hunting to anonymous multifamily buildings.

WHAT YOU CAN RENT

There are apartments and there are apartments, and indeed, as you begin shopping around you will find that your three and a half rooms with bath can come in a variety of structural styles.

- *The High-Rise Building* Usually with high rent as well, these are often of new construction, but sometimes can be old, genteel dwellings. Advantages: perhaps a doorman, diversity of tenants, opportunity to meet new people, maybe fancy address. Disadvantages: in addition to often high rent, sometimes shoddy construction; can be impersonal, even unfriendly, instead of the congenial place you may have been seeking.

- *The Brownstone* A row house of any construction, but generically called "brownstone." Brownstones are usually found ringing a downtown area. Advantages: interesting architectural details such as high ceilings, moldings, perhaps a fireplace or two; sense of living in a home rather than an apartment building. Disadvantages: the area in which the house is situated may be a little (or a lot) on the rough side; in nicer parts of town, rent can be very high; fewer modern conveniences like large closets, second bath, etc.

- *The Apartment in a Private Home* How this looks, and how much you enjoy the experience, will depend on the house and neighborhood and the virtues and faults of the owner, who is likely to live just above or below you. Advantages: again, a homelike atmosphere, and maybe even a yard to yourselves. Disadvantages: the landlord may drive you to distraction over every petty little thing (of course, living in a private home does not necessarily mean surrendering your privacy to a nosy landlord). If you can, talk to the previous tenants, who may be able to tell you their experiences about living there.

- *The Single-Family House* Renting an entire house is often possible, frequently at a cost lower than a small apartment in a good section of town. Advantages: a chance to try out homeowning before signing the mortgage papers; all that space. Disadvantages: maybe *too* much space; could be an absentee landlord living hundreds of miles away, making contact for repairs difficult; a certain amount of responsibility on your part: you'll have to shovel snow, cut the grass, etc.; there could be substantial commuting costs.

- *The Garden Apartment*   Usually located in the suburbs, complexes in which these apartments can be found consist of one- or two-story buildings sometimes surrounding an area of greenery or social amenities set aside for use by the tenants. Advantages: all those extra niceties that may come with the lease—lively social program, a pool, tennis court, clubhouse, free parking, laundry room, etc. Disadvantages: Can *you* think of any? One point, however: You may want to take note of your would-be fellow tenants when checking out these complexes. Some seem to attract tenants with young children; others draw an overwhelming number of young singles or retirees. Still, there are certainly many such communities that contain a mix of all types.

- *The Loft*   Trendy lifestyle. You rent a floor or part of a floor in a building that has previously been used for manufacturing purposes. Advantages: lots of space, sometimes the ability to lay out rooms any way you want, or just keep that vast square footage open. Disadvantages: like brownstones, loft buildings can sometimes be found in areas of town that are not particularly safe. Also, in a loft you may have to spend plenty to make your apartment attractive and bring it up to local code requirements for residential living if those have not yet been met. Do you want to do this if you rent?

- *Walk-Ups*   Usually plain, modest structures, or large tenements. Whether you want to live in one may depend on its condition. Perhaps the owner has renovated the units, or at least keeps up maintenance. Advantages: may be a good deal if the rehab was substantial; rents frequently lower than those in comparable fancy buildings on the same block. Disadvantages: no elevator (usually one is required by law for buildings five or six stories or more; the renovated building may just fall short of that requirement, so you'd have to trudge up the steps); maybe only minor renovation has been done, with old problems just below the surface.

- *Government-Subsidized Housing*   Comes in all varieties of buildings, with rents all or in part underwritten by the government—either federal or local agencies. Income requirements for admittance, and other restrictions as well.

Dani and Steve did their shopping well, visiting a number of apartment buildings and garden complexes, since they had confined their search to the suburbs. Ultimately, they selected a garden development some twenty years old. They took the first-floor apartment in a two-story block with four units. There were nine of these buildings forming the community, all ringing a pool area. Their monthly rent turned out to be $50 more than the two had counted on, but they decided that was a small price to pay for a great address and the pool, which they knew they would use often.

Dani and Steve had lived in a couple of apartments over the years, and so knew which questions to ask when applying to become tenants. (See checklist on page 30.)

The couple's questions were answered to their satisfaction, and they agreed to take the apartment. Next: the legalities.

Considering the Lease

Granted, this is a somewhat frightening document. Any legal document usually is. Most leases are standard forms printed by the millions and sold in stationery stores. You should know they are usually written by lawyers' groups, so they stress the rights of the property owner, but tenants' rights are mentioned too.

Read over the document, taking particular note of the passages that have been typed or written in, and of clauses covering specific conditions that may apply to you. For instance, typewritten parts will include your name and address, the amount of rent, the date your occupancy begins. Which of you signs the lease? If you are not married yet, both of you will sign. If you are moving into your husband's apartment, be sure to have your name added to his lease. Add his name, of course, if he is moving into your place.

Specific changes should be written in before you sign a lease, but sometimes circumstances change *after* you have moved in; then a new clause can be written in and initialed by both owner and tenant. Or perhaps a letter from management can serve as your protection.

For example, if the owner or manager has agreed to paint before you move in, that clause can be added to the lease prior to signing. If, after you have been living there a while, you want to wallpaper a room, and the landlord says yes, get that permission in writing. Papering changes an apartment, and you are not likely to want to strip it off before you move. Life does change, even during the course of a one-year lease. Once you are in an apartment, you may want to make some alterations or bring certain situations to the attention of the landlord. (For instance, if there is no room in the apartment or hallway to store your bicycles, but plenty of space for them in the locked basement laundry room, you may want to get permission to park them there.) By all means ask if you would like a reasonable change made—and get permission in writing.

Have a pet you want to bring to the apartment with you? That permission may be entered as a clause in the lease. A word of caution here. If the lease does not mention pets at all, it is generally conceded that they are allowed. But don't assume they are just because you see other people walking dogs in the complex. Maybe these dog owners are visitors and do not live there, or perhaps the no-pets ruling has only recently gone into effect and tenants in residence at the time have been allowed to keep, but not replace, their animals. How *many* you may have is debatable. Two is usually not a problem, but it depends on how much of a nuisance they are to fellow tenants, and whether your neighbors complain. Seven cats may be five too many!

Important: In the lease, make a note of problems you have found in the apartment, so that you will not be blamed for them when you move out. An air-conditioner that does not work, for example, or a major tear in the linoleum is worth noting.

In some parts of the country you may not even be offered a lease; this usually happens when you rent in an owner's home with only a unit or two to let. An oral agreement is generally binding, especially after a rent payment has been accepted. The oral agreement does not protect you against rent increases, however. And while you're not locked into disadvantageous lease provisions if you have no written document, you may not be able to get the landlord's promise in writing to paint the place—or to do anything else—either. For the most part you have the same protection as a leaseholder, but without a lease a landlord can often get rid of you with thirty days' notice if he chooses, although you can move with similar notice and no penalty.

Where you are presented with a lease, don't expect a term longer than one or two years. The advantage of a long-term lease is not that you won't have rent increases. Your rent may well rise at the end of each year, according to statutes where you live. But if you plan to stay a while in that building or complex, the longer lease gives you some protection against the landlord's whims.

BREAKING A LEASE

Although they did fine with most questions to their landlord, Dani and Steve forgot one: what would happen if they had to break their lease. A transfer could come up for either one of them, although neither was particularly seeking one. Still, if the offer was good . . . There is nothing to stop you from moving out before the term of your lease has expired—except that you are breaking a contract and may be held responsible for its terms. The owner could track you down and sue you for the portion of rent you owe, plus expenses he incurred in reclaiming that money. It would be better for you to find out how to break a lease—legally.

Perhaps you can sublet (see "Short-Term Subletting," below). Maybe your apartment is in such a hot market the landlord will have no trouble renting your unit and will be amenable to your leaving early if a satisfactory tenant is found (be sure to have that in writing when you leave, of course).

You have a couple of other choices as well.

There is something known as the "build/buy" clause that can be written into a lease. If you plan to build or buy a home but aren't sure when it will be ready for occupancy, you can try to persuade the landlord to insert this clause into your lease, allowing you to move out when your home is ready, even if it's before the lease ends. A similar clause may be inserted if you're pretty sure you will be taking a new job some miles away and, again, will have to back out of a lease. While trying to add such a clause is a good idea, it is not likely to work in a market where vacancies are few. If you try either option, and the landlord agrees, you will not be able to move out immediately. You'll still have to give notice, the length of which is negotiable, and can be as little as a month or two.

If you find you want to move, or must move, in the middle of a lease, and you've made no arrangement with the landlord, the building owner may not want to let you off the hook even if you're willing to leave behind the security deposit. Perhaps you might sweeten the pot by forfeiting the security deposit *plus* another month's rent. If he agrees to these or other conditions, be sure to get the agreement in writing.

If you have been a good tenant, have taken care of your unit and paid rent on time, a letter to the landlord explaining your reason for having to move on—a job transfer, the serious illness of a family member—might help your case, and you may avoid the actions mentioned above. Send the letter by certified mail so that you have proof it was delivered. Depending on the landlord's sentiments and the rental market in your community, you may be wished well and sent on your way.

The very last resort for breaking a lease is a tricky little device known as the "constructive eviction," whereby you move out if living conditions in your apartment are so unimaginably horrible you can no longer tolerate staying there. Let's say you have seen rats in the building. Or, despite your repeated letters to the landlord, noise from the adjoining apartment is making your life miserable. While this can be one legal way out of a lease, it's a tough one and shouldn't even be considered without an attorney guiding you through the process.

Dani and Steve could have mentioned the possibility of a job transfer to their landlord when they signed their two-year lease, but since that possibility was a long shot, it was better not to. You don't want to turn off a building owner during a first meeting.

A BABY? MAYBE

If you move into an apartment building or complex and sign a clause that states, more or less, "We understand no children are allowed in this building," what happens if you should become pregnant? Can you be evicted?

The question of children born to couples living in "adults-only" communities is a complicated one, and is being brought before the courts in some states. In California, for example, a couple tested the rule as it applied to their condominium community in the courts and it was found to be illegal. In a few other states, a new baby has meant eviction and the parents have had to sell their condo or mobile home.

As a renter in a building or community that has this policy, you may be allowed to stay for a while, but your lease may not be renewed.

Keep all this in mind as you apartment-shop. This might be another question to ask your local tenant organization.

ALTERATIONS AND REPAIRS

This can be a difficult area. If the place needs lots of work, clarify with the landlord how repairs and payment for them are to be handled. You don't want to put in your sweat, tears, and maybe big bucks fixing up the place, only to be hit by a rent increase once your landlord sees his newly renovated apartment. Perhaps he will offer to pay for supplies and raise your rent gradually over a specified period of time, or not raise it at all (again, for a specified period of time) in return for your labor. Naturally, you must have this spelled out in a clause in the lease.

Be sure you are clear about who is to do what in terms of maintenance and repairs, too, either by reading the lease or by asking questions of the landlord or rental agent. Sometimes you can get everything that's broken fixed, and sometimes you can't—and that's often just the way it is when you live in an apartment (a lot more about this headache is in Chapter 3).

RENEWAL

Your lease may have a clause saying you will be allowed to renew automatically, assuming you have been a satisfactory tenant. You are free not to renew, of course, and so is your landlord, unless your state has some protection against ouster by the building owner. Some lease renewals—i.e., signing a new lease after your current one expires—mean an automatic rent increase, while in others the landlord can raise the rent or not. Usually there is no mention of increases in the lease itself. If your lease contains an automatic renewal clause and you don't plan to stay another year, you'd better be quick to notify management before you're automatically—and legally—tied up for that time. Also, the wording may be such that if you do not *notify* the owner of your intent to *stay,* the lease is canceled. Read your lease well before renewal time so that you know what your situation is.

HUNTING IN A TIGHT MARKET

- Register with building management companies that handle several apartment houses with hundreds of units around town. Saves legwork.

- Consider hunting early and adding your name to a waiting list. It only takes sixty to ninety days for a vacancy to occur at most places.

- Try apartment-finding services that *do not charge you a fee*. These are offered by landlords' organizations in some sections of the country. Avoid the ones that charge if you can!

- Work the neighborhood in which you are interested. Talk to the woman sweeping her sidewalk; become friendly with the mail carrier on that route, who is likely to know of apartment vacancies and even who is planning to move. Talk to building superintendents. (Yes, you should give them "a little something" if an apartment pans out. Depending on the part of the country where you live, and the neighborhood where you're looking, that could be anywhere from $20 to $100 or more.)

- Check notices on bulletin boards at supermarkets, the library—any public building or store where many of them are posted. Don't bother putting up your own Apartment Wanted notice. In a tight market, no landlord has to go to the trouble of reading notices.

- It's best to shop around the latter third of the month, worst around the first. Fall has plenty of turnover activity, while summer is slower.

- Carrying credentials with you so that you can present them to a prospective landlord on the spot may get you an apartment. These include credit cards, driver's license, maybe even a résumé (yours and/or your fiancé's/husband's). Personal references can help, too, when a building owner wants to make a quick decision.

- Remember that in an extremely tight market you are not likely to find the apartment of your fantasies. You'll be settling, not selecting. But make the most of this first home, and remember the great stories you can relate about your somewhat cramped lifestyle in the flat above the pinball alley. What fun!

SHORT-TERM SUBLETTING

Let's say your husband is planning to take a summer course abroad, and you'll be going with him. Or maybe you're renting a summer place and will commute to work directly from the beach house. Why not pick up a few dollars subletting your apartment while it is vacant? you reason. Not all leases allow tenants to sublet, and when they do, the wording may read like this: "The tenant agrees not to sublet this lease without the landlord's consent, which consent will not be unreasonably withheld." It is always better to notify the landlord if you plan to offer your place to someone else. Some building owners may be just itching to get rid of tenants so they can raise the rent for that unit, or perhaps convert the building, or sell it vacant to a new owner. He or she may be delighted to catch you in a lease violation.

The really short-term sublets—say, two or three weeks in the summer—are a gray area. Is this your cousin coming to stay in your place at no charge? Or a paying stranger? Some tenants go ahead and find a subtenant, conveniently forgetting to alert management. A handsome tip may ensure the doorman's or superintendent's cooperation. But this is a gamble, and you will have to decide whether the odds work in your favor.

Questions resolved, you and the landlord (or his representative) sign the lease, you are handed your copy, and you put it away— in a safe place, where it will probably remain untouched for years. It makes a nice memento of your first place as a married couple, though.

IS THIS THE PLACE FOR YOU?
A CHECKLIST

What is the rent and what does it include—utilities, recreational areas, etc.? When is it due? To whom do you send the check? Is there a grace period for payment? Are there late charges attached after a certain time? (Usually there will be, in larger complexes, where, beyond the third or fourth day of the month, tenants are charged 3 to 6 percent.) Can the rent rise before your lease is up? Are there rent-control laws in your community? (You can check your local or statewide tenant organization.)

What period of time does the lease cover? (One or two years is most common.) What happens if you break the lease? Will you lose your security deposit? Do you have the option of subletting?

Notice the exterior of the building and the grounds. Are they clean and well maintained, or could the grass stand a mowing and the building use a fresh coat of paint?

Is there an elevator? Is it self-service, or is there an operator? On duty twenty-four hours?

If there is a doorman, is he around or does he always seem to be on a break? Does he let you in if you've forgotten your key? If not, who does? Is the lobby area well lighted? What about locks on outside doors? How many entrances are there? Are they all secured?

As you notice your fellow tenants going in and out of the building, do you think you would fit in with them? Or is there too much of an age or lifestyle difference between you?

What about parking? Is there a garage available? At an extra cost? If you must park on nearby streets, is it difficult to find space? Is it a dangerous area?

Does the refrigerator come with the apartment? What about the dishwasher and/or clothes washer and dryer, if you see those appliances?

Check the laundry room, if there is one. Is it neat? Do all the machines work? What about the safety factor in that area? If there is no laundry space, will the landlord allow you to install a washer and dryer? If not, where is the nearest laundromat?

How do you dispose of trash? Is there an incinerator?

Is the building wired for cable television? Will the landlord allow it to be installed?

In looking through specific apartments, be sure to consider the following:

- Wiring. Is it adequate without having to run several extension cords? Two outlets per room is the minimum you should expect. Check the light switches and doorbell, too.

- Is there enough storage space? (No, there never is, but look around the apartment for potential areas in which to stow gear or install shelves.) Can you use part of the basement for storage?

- Is the apartment clean and freshly painted? (Regulations governing painting vary from one community to another and depend on the number of units in a building, but you may learn you are entitled to a fresh paint job every three years.) If the landlord does not intend to repaint for you, will he deduct the cost of materials from an upcoming rent check if you do the job yourself?

- What is the condition of the floors? Are there ceiling leaks? Chunks of plaster missing here and there?

- Visit twice if you can—day and evening—to see if you can hear your neighbors more than you would like, and whether the street noise will bother you.

- What are the rooms' dimensions? Will they accommodate the furniture you already have? Does the place feel large enough for the two of you? What about entertaining? Room for overnight guests?

- This may seem obvious, but talk over just how you see the rooms functioning. He may automatically assume that small second bedroom will be an office–computer center—you may feel it's a guest room. Can you agree on how to use the space available?

- It never hurts to stop a tenant in or outside the building to ask how well maintained the place is and if there are any other problems—security, say, or perhaps talk of a condominium conversion (which may interest you greatly or totally turn you off that place). Folks are usually genial when approached for their opinion, and of course it's all off the record. No need to ask their names.

3

LIFE AS A TENANT

"Hon, is that water dripping under the kitchen sink? Better call the super."
"Two months now and still no refund on our security deposit. This is ridiculous!"
"If that guy doesn't stop with that horn, I'm going up there and . . ."

Ah, life as a tenant.

You may think that because you are a renter, repairs, maintenance chores, and the like are not your concern. You will just pick up the phone and call whoever is supposed to handle those petty annoyances and *snap!* the job will be done. Of course it will. Actually, watching things break, tracking down the proper contact for repairs, waiting for workers to show up, making more phone calls, having the job done wrong—all contribute to the reality of apartment life, which is that you really must know how to launch a proper campaign to get repairs made. Or letters answered. Or problems solved. If you don't, you will be at the mercy of your landlord, your fellow tenants, and other outside forces, all of whom can seem almost conspiratorial in making your life miserable. Here is how to handle yourselves in the most common areas of dissension.

Broadly Speaking

When you moved in, you should have been given the name of the person or office to call when things go wrong. Perhaps it is the building superintendent, the management company located across town, or maybe the rental office just downstairs, adjacent to the lobby. In an owner-occupied home, your landlord, of course, is only a floor or two away.

That individual or company should be called first; if your problem is not addressed, or your phone calls are not returned within a reasonable period of time (three or four days), follow up your complaint in writing, keeping a copy of your letter. Be pleasant in the note, and businesslike. You may need this written correspondence if the complaint grows into something serious one day, like a lawsuit. Oral promises *can* be honored in court, but how much better to have your communications, dated and with your opponent's response, right there in black and white. If there *is* no response, that says something, too.

But somewhere between everybody's doing nothing and your suing everyone in sight come a few other possible solutions that can be much easier on the nerves.

Who's Going to Fix It?

The law is complicated in the area of who fixes what in an apartment. Generally, building owners must repair anything they promised to fix in the lease or in a written or oral agreement. They must also provide rudimentary services, such as heat and hot water, garbage collection, repairs to the roof and walls. They must keep the public areas, such as hallways, in repair. Most states have what is known as a "warranty of habitability" law, whereby your landlord must provide a certain standard of service, including the services mentioned above, and, in some buildings, elevator service, air conditioning, and electronic security systems. This means you can gripe about "habitability" when you have no heat in February but not when the landlord does a poor job of painting the place.

Tenants are responsible for keeping things shipshape in their own apartments and for repairing damage caused by their own negligence or carelessness.

Malfunctions that come under the heading of housing code violations are certainly serious, but here, too, you could find yourself with a retaliatory eviction attempt (more about that later in this chapter) and the landlord handed a mere $25 fine. The outcome depends on the buildings department where you live and whether they enforce laws strictly.

Sadly for tenants, many repairs fall into the gray area where no one is responsible for making them. If you want something fixed, you can ask the landlord to do it. If he says no, you can do the job yourself at your own expense. Nonresponsibility works both ways. You do not have to make certain repairs the landlord asks for. Also in this amorphous category is damage to an apartment resulting from natural disasters, such as flood, fire, or hurricane. Unless the lease says otherwise, neither of you can be held accountable.

But let's say the toilet in your powder room floods. You've made two calls to the building management office and have received no response. Can you arrange to have the repair made yourself and deduct the cost from next month's rent check? Perhaps. Here's where you need to know landlord-tenant law in your area. Check with your statewide tenants' association, or one in your town, or a local legal-aid office. Since the repair to be made is necessary to restore satisfactory health and safety conditions, and is not a cosmetic one, you are likely to be on more solid ground if you want to make the repair yourselves.

Still, write to the building owner, keeping a copy of your letter. Mention the need to have the toilet fixed, and that you will see to it yourselves if management does not. Allow a reasonable time for a response, a time that may be stipulated in local or state law. You must have proof that you tried to reach the building owner.

Still no answer? If the law is on your side, then go ahead and call the plumber (you may be required to get two estimates, accepting the lower one). Keep copies of the estimates and receipts of the bills. Subtract the amount you have spent from the next month's rent, attaching the estimates, bills, and receipts. Copies of all of this should go into your files. If the landlord should claim you did not pay your rent in full and files a court case to collect or tries to evict you, you have all the documents you need for your side of the case. The above is a scenario that *may* work for you, and probably will—but state laws vary. Always seek guidance first from an attorney or the local tenants' organization.

A REMINDER

Don't forget renter's insurance. Your landlord carries insurance for the building itself and the common areas. He is not responsible for your furnishings. Look into a policy covering your possessions against burglary, fire, and other calamities, plus liability coverage in the event someone is hurt in your apartment or outside your unit from injuries caused by you.

Another feature of tenant insurance is limited protection for items that may be stolen from your car while you are transporting them from your home, and payment for living costs (hotel, meals) if your apartment becomes uninhabitable for a short time because of, say, a burst pipe.

Shop around for the best policy. Premium rates vary, of course, but you should be able to purchase adequate coverage for $125 to $200 a year.

More serious repairs (plaster is falling from the ceiling due to a leak from the roof above you) may be solved by withholding rent, but here, too, you need advice from a tenants' organization or a real estate attorney. You will probably have to keep paying rent, but can deposit it into an escrow account until you are satisfied that your apartment has been fixed.

If problems with repairs are building-wide, you may want to band together with your fellow tenants to form a tenants' association. A building-wide rent strike can be very effective, since you have the strength of numbers. But again, that major caution: Do it only after you have been apprised of your responsibilities and rights—and the landlord's.

Can We Hang a Picture, Maybe Two?

Another area of tenant life you may well have concerns about is just how much "like home" you can make your three and a half rooms with bath. Can you hang pictures on the wall? Absolutely. You are not renting a monk's cell, after all, and should it come to that, any judge would deem a reasonable number of nail holes in a wall, well, reasonable.

Still, the very large nails left when bookshelves are removed are another matter, and so are the chips that fall from the plaster when you hit and miss. Those gaps and large nail holes after you remove them must be filled in when you move. This is an example of structural damage. (Ordinary nail holes from pictures usually do not have to be filled in.)

One way to get around restrictions is to replace and save. If you don't like the lighting fixture over the kitchen table, replace it, but save the one that came with your unit. When you move, put it back up. Same with switch plates, patio furniture, or any furnishings you'd rather not live with during your time there.

Wallpapering, exposing a brick wall, laying tile or linoleum—any decorating more than painting (and then only an innocuous color—not navy blue or Chinese red!) may be a job that changes the apartment radically. Proceed here only after talking it over with the building owner. Perhaps he or she will feel your contribution adds to the value of the place, and so will approve your plans. If you intend to take with you any installations you're thinking of making—built-in bookcases, for example—that are also likely to improve the appearance of the apartment, make sure the owner understands your intentions. Drag out the lease and add a clause which states that you are allowed to do what you plan—initialed by both parties, of course. Or ask for a letter of permission from the owner that you can keep in your files.

Uninvited Visitors: Two-Legged Variety

You come home one evening and something's just not quite right. Wasn't that chair flush against the wall, not so close to the end table? Or, more ominous yet, you find a cigarette butt in the toilet, and you don't smoke. Who has been here? Heart thumping, you run to the bureau drawer where you keep spare cash. It's there. Nothing else in the apartment seems to have been disturbed. So what happened?

What you have probably experienced is a visit by the building owner. He may have come in to inspect the apartment, make repairs or to show the apartment (if you are moving) to another set of tenants or to someone interested in buying the building.

You may not like the idea, but the landlord is entitled by law to enter your apartment for those reasons, and to give a key to the person or company he considers his agent, such as a management company or the building super. Tenants are entitled to their privacy, however. Landlords usually must give twenty-four to seventy-two hours' notice before coming in. Naturally, emergencies require no advance warning, and that's all to the good. If 5B's overflowing bathtub is loosening the ceiling in your apartment, you'd want the landlord to enter 4B pretty darn quickly.

Uninvited Visitors: Four-Legged (or More!) Variety

You say you have bugs in your apartment? That's just a euphemism for roaches, isn't it? Maybe you've seen them before in your previous apartments. Or perhaps you've moved from your parents' single-family home, a lovely place where the only pests were the occasional summer housefly and your kid brother; roaches, you thought, lived with those who weren't too familiar with a broom or a mop.

Roaches, as many of us eventually learn, can be found in just about any multifamily building, from the flossiest address to the meanest. And once they have established a beachhead, it's tough to see the backs of them.

Your building may have a monthly extermination service, which is good, if the exterminator manages to get into all apartments. By all means, allow him into yours. Even if he skips a few of your neighbors, it's a wise move, since the beasties are more likely to gravitate toward untreated areas than to the fort you have tried to make of your unit.

If the building has no regular extermination service, the tenants can band together and ask the owner to provide one. If he says no (and he is probably not required to pay for that service by law, although you can check with your local health department), you can all contribute to have the place exterminated. The cost is minimal. An initial cleanout of one apartment can run from $35 to $50, with $10 or $15 charged for each monthly follow-up call. If the whole building is involved, the cleanout may be less costly.

MERRY CHRISTMAS, MR. DOORMAN
HAPPY HOLIDAYS, MR. SUPER

Why is the building staff so friendly these days? It must be the approach of the holiday season. Time to start thinking of your, shall we say, seasonal gratuity.

If you are in a building or complex where tenants band together to present a "pool gift" to the staff, and collect among their neighbors by passing the hat, you are off the hook as far as guessing about tipping is concerned.

If that's not the situation, asking your fellow tenants what they give may not be much help. Some will inflate those figures, wanting you to think they are more generous than they are. Others will not even discuss the matter.

If your building has a tenants' association, by all means ask them for suggestions.

In some complexes run by management companies, you may be sent a sheet before the holidays, listing the names of the staff. You might call that office for hints about how much to tip, but don't be surprised if they choose not to be specific.

A general guideline for Christmas is to tip a total of 10 to 15 percent of your monthly rent divided among the staff. In what ratio? If left totally to your own devices, here are a few suggestions, which cover the smallest, most modest of buildings as well as the most posh.

- The superintendent, no matter what his level of competence, comes in for the largest sum. You want this man on your side, especially when it's 101 degrees in July and your bedroom air-conditioner needs repair. Tip $15 to $100.

- Handymen, doormen, elevator operators, garage attendants: $10 to $50. Some of these people are tipped during the year as well.

- The behind-the-scenes maintenance staff. The management company or your own tenants' association can tell you who they are. This could be covered by a "pool gift" if there are several of these employees. They are each usually given less than the more visible staff people mentioned above.

Getting rid of roaches completely may still seem a state of bliss yet to be reached. Between exterminator visits you may want to try a home remedy that often works—sprinkling boric acid around, out of reach of pets or children. Pour it lavishly behind the sink, refrigerator, dishwasher, under the bathroom sink, in your laundry area, if you have one. Repeat periodically, when it looks dried and stale.

Silverfish are dark brown bugs about an inch and a half long that seem to like undisturbed areas such as basements and attics. They aren't often found in living areas, preferring to hide in trunks, unopened boxes of books, and the like. They feed on wallpaper and books. Wash the areas where you find them, and then spray with a supermarket pesticide.

Pantry pests (weevils and beetles) can be treated the same way—wash and then spray. But don't spray if you have roaches, too. Sprays tend to bring roaches out of hiding, making *that* condition worse, especially in the pantry area. Store food that comes in bags, like sugar and flour, and opened boxes of rice in tight-lidded jars or canisters.

The Noise Is Driving Me C-r-a-z-y!

You probably have a sentence in your lease stating that you are entitled to "quiet enjoyment of the premises." But how are you supposed to quietly enjoy them, you question angrily, with all the noise coming from the apartment next door (or upstairs or down the hall)? Your nerves are frazzled, you hate spending time in your own apartment, and yet you do not want to knock on the door of the offending tenant because one never knows what to expect from confrontations. What to do? You and your husband have called the police twice. Once it worked and the bloody stereo was turned down for the remainder of the evening, but two nights later it blared again. Another call to the police brought peace for only a few more evenings. You don't want to bother with them again.

This is a toughie because noise pollution is not a priority of landlords or enforcement officials, yet you are *entitled* to that quiet enjoyment.

1. Don't approach the other tenant yourself initially. Write your building owner a letter (keeping a copy for yourselves, of course) setting forth your complaint and asking him to contact the tenant for some resolution. He may be reluctant to get involved, but remember you have the law on your side. Your letter might read like this:

> Dear Mr. Landlord:
> We are tenants in apartment 6B at your building, the Lotus Leaf Arms. We have been having serious problems over the last month with noise emanating from our neighbor's apartment 6C. The stereo plays loudly from around 8:00 p.m. until well after midnight, sometimes five nights a week. We believe this violates *our* rights as tenants and would appreciate your contacting this individual and asking him to turn down the volume. We have discussed this with other tenants on the floor, and believe some of them may also have contacted you.
> If you'd like to talk to us, we can be reached in the evening at 555-5867. John Jones's work number is 555-9048; Kathy Jones can be reached during the day at 555-4768.
> Would you handle this, please?
>
> Sincerely yours,
>
> John Jones
> Kathy Jones

2. If you get no response from the owner, you might approach the other tenant yourselves, trying to be polite and tactful. That can sometimes work, although again, the peace may last only a short time. At the first sign of any unpleasantness, however, back off and leave. This could be a person you would not want to deal with at any length.

3. You can engage a lawyer specializing in landlord-tenant law, or even noise pollution, a pricy solution.

4. You can further spur your landlord into action by withholding rent. This should be done after talking with the tenants' association in your area, of course, or even with a lawyer.

Try to bolster any case you make, whether it's in a written grievance or a court appearance, by keeping track of dates and times of the noise and, if you can, by tape-recording the stereo, drums, barking dog, or other noise.

About Evictions

When was the last time you saw a renter with his or her furniture on the sidewalk, obviously evicted by the landlord? Probably never, right? That type of eviction belongs to the old days, or perhaps even old novels. But eviction *does* occur, for any number of reasons. Sometimes you have control over being ousted by the landlord—by paying rent faithfully each month, for example—and sometimes you do not—a retaliatory eviction, say (see below).

Eviction laws differ from one state to another, but today the possibility of finding one's possessions on the street has virtually disappeared. Still, you should know what *could* get you evicted.

• Nonpayment of rent or any other violation of the lease, such as not keeping the property in good condition (*how* "good" is open to the judge's interpretation), keeping pets when the lease forbids them, etc. Usually you will be given a chance to correct violations and, if you do, will be allowed to stay.

- The landlord wants your apartment for his own use or for use by a member of his family, which may be allowed by law. Naturally, you will have to be given a certain amount of notice.

- Interfering with the comfort and safety of the landlord and/or the other tenants—like making the noise mentioned above.

- Behaving illegally—dealing drugs from the apartment, say.

- Not allowing the owner "reasonable access" to your unit, for repairs, emergencies, and the like.

- The landlord wants to demolish the building, or is planning extensive renovations, perhaps switching it to a condominium or cooperative. In this instance, you may have legal protection of some sort against a quick ouster.

Generally, these are the most common causes for eviction. There is one other—retaliatory eviction, whereby the landlord tries to get rid of a tenant who has become a "problem" by complaining to authorities about building code violations, organizing other tenants, or forming a city-wide tenant union. Most states now forbid retaliatory evictions, however.

Landlords must follow a set procedure if they want a tenant out. In most states they are forbidden to place a lock on the tenant's door, or change his lock, to keep him from the premises. The landlord must go to court for an eviction order, showing that there is a basis for taking that step. The landlord cannot hold a tenant's possessions for nonpayment of rent either. Tenants can call in the police, and sue him or her for damages.

If you ever find yourself in the position of being threatened with eviction, take it seriously and learn your rights by contacting your nearest tenants' organization, or the state office that handles landlord-tenant relations.

After reading this litany of potential problems in apartment living, you can see that your best allies are likely to be your local or statewide tenants' organizations, and your state Department of Community Affairs, which may have a landlord-tenant bureau. That office usually publishes a booklet answering dozens of questions that will occur to you—or be presented to you—during your life as a renter. It would be wise to contact the appropriate state office at the first sign of trouble from a landlord, and keep that phone number handy.

IF YOUR BUILDING IS GOING CONDO (OR CO-OP)

What happens to you as a tenant if you have already received word that your building is about to undergo conversion to a condominium (or to a cooperative, though the conversion to this housing style is less common)? If you do not want to buy your unit, you may have some protection from laws in your state; you may at least be allowed to stay until the term of your lease expires, or be given as much as three years' notice before eviction.

No doubt your building will organize quickly once the word is out, and you will know your rights soon enough. They vary widely from one state to another. In some states you can cancel your lease when notified about a conversion plan, and move out with thirty days' notice.

Should you buy your unit? You may be given first crack at it, either by state law or by the sponsor—the individual or group that owns the building now and is overseeing the conversion. Maybe your tenants' group has negotiated a nice insider's price, too, well below what comparable condos are selling for in the area where you live. If it is an adequate apartment, but not your dream place, you may still want to consider buying. At a good price, perhaps with attractive financing arranged by an eager-to-convert sponsor, you may have an excellent starter home. Stay for a short time and sell at a handsome profit. Then you'll have a nice chunk of cash to put down on the home you *really* want. Just make sure the apartment is resalable (take into account the building it's in as well as the apartment itself), an important consideration when buying any home.

For more information about your rights in a conversion, contact your state Attorney General's Office.

4

FURNISHING
YOUR HOME—
NOW
AND WITH
LONG-RANGE
GOALS
IN MIND

He will not part with the huge, decidedly unattractive bookcase he has lugged from college dormitory to studio walk-up to your new home together. *You* can't understand why he makes a face at your much-loved Laura Ashley fabrics and calls them "ditsy." *He* says he doesn't know much about art, but he knows what he likes—and what he likes appalls you. *You* come to your new home with two cat-clawed upholstered chairs he's ready to toss (fortunately for the relationship, he won't pitch the two felines responsible for the tatters). Can this new marriage be saved?

Perhaps your situation is not a bounty of too many possessions to quibble about. Maybe you are both coming from your folks' home or a college room, and have virtually nothing with which to furnish a home. An excellent opportunity to spend your money on what you *both* like, but where do you start?

Still another scenario may describe you. You are expecting a job switch to another town at any time, or perhaps one of you is in the military, or will be taking a postgraduate or professional course. In any event, you are headed for a new locale for just a year or two and do not want to haul too much in the way of furnishings with you. You will want to make yourselves as comfortable as possible, but inexpensively—very inexpensively.

Decorating a first home together usually means (1) each of you bringing in at least a few furnishings of your own; (2) a budget, either because there is no money for furnishings or because you are saving for a house or some other purpose; and (3) the two of you are talking, almost from Day One, about when you will move from that first place and where you will look next.

So the challenge is to create a chic, rather temporary home out of a few start-up materials and a budget that is not luxurious. You want to be doing some long-range planning, too.

It can all be done!

Thinking It Through

There is no way to tell you specifically what to buy and how to arrange it, however. A home is a personal statement. No one but you and your husband can divine what possessions and collections are particularly important to you and how you envision the home you share as husband and wife. You will have to decide about styles, space allotments, and purchases yourselves, taking into account the size and dimensions of your apartment, what furnishings you have to work with now, a merging of your separate tastes, your checkbook balance (and credit card limit, plus perhaps wedding-gift checks), and some ideas of how long you plan to remain in this first home.

The initial step—and this applies to everybody, regardless of their income or how much they need to buy—is to decide how much you can spend on decorating. Next, work out which elements of the project are most important to you (the sofa? carpeting throughout? some area rugs? art? wall storage units?).

Finally, work out a time frame. Will this budget you have just created cover the entire decorating process, or does it constitute only Phase One? If money is a factor—and, of course, it is likely to be—it is a good idea to plan one major purchase for each room: a sofa, for example, for the living room, and maybe a brass bed for the bedroom. These ought to be quality items, ones you can build a room around as the years go by. Once you have pinpointed the principal expenses, you can decide what extras might be included in the initial stage.

Looking ahead is important when purchasing furniture; most of it is expensive these days, so you don't want anything you'll tire of quickly. A sofa should last many years, so look for one that might work in your next home as well as this first one. Think classic, not avant-garde. Your tastes are likely to change even over the next couple of years, and you do not want to be stuck with a $1,000 mistake that may have reflected your taste, in terms of decor, when you were twenty-seven, but is a far cry from you at thirty-one. On the other hand, there is no need to play it *too* safe, buying the boring little beige sofa because it is likely to last through eternity and beige is such a stable color. Experiment a little, especially as you are now blending your style and his. Go for color, too. But always ask yourself how soon you are likely to tire of what now excites you.

A good area carpet will travel well through successive homes, and one can be purchased whose style may well reflect your taste at every subsequent stage of your life—in one room or another. A bed frame with a top-of-the-line mattress and box spring is an important purchase, but a matching bedroom "suite" is not, and indeed is less stylish than mixing and matching pieces.

Odd tables and chairs, and furniture for the kitchen, can be purchased without considering longevity. Do not buy cheap furniture, however. You will soon hate it and look for the first opportunity to rid yourselves of it. There is an applicable Dutch proverb: A cheap buy is an expensive buy.

WHAT'S YOUR STYLE?

Maybe it's still evolving. But while you furnish your first home, even if it's done with hand-me-downs, you will see a certain look emerging. Your new acquisitions, the fusion of your taste and his, your color choices and furniture placement—all will translate into a style. Which of the following is you right now?

ECLECTIC   This is a combination of different designs that has come to mean a little of this and a little of that, which may well constitute your inventory at this stage. High-style pieces blending with more traditional furnishings can work well if a room is thoughtfully put together.

TRADITIONAL   Rooms decorated in this manner are rather formal, with furniture styles and window treatments suggestive of the seventeenth and eighteenth centuries. Williamsburg reproductions are one example.

DRAMATIC   You will know these rooms when you walk into them. The owner has made unique, even experimental use of color. Lighting, furniture, and fabrics are sleek and spare.

CONTEMPORARY–HIGH TECH   Not quite as strong a statement as Dramatic, these rooms are usually minimally furnished, with clean lines and monochromatic or neutral tones. Chrome and glass are likely to take the place of wood; blinds instead of curtains. Fabrics can be tweed, suede, or leather.

ROMANTIC   The key to these interiors is lushness, with rooms featuring soft lights, gauzy or lace window curtains, and furniture—like wicker—that has a light look. Some Victorian styles can be lovely and very romantic.

COUNTRY   These rooms are considered "warm" or "cozy," never formal. Whether American, French, or English country, the furniture style is, on the whole, more sturdy than that used in traditional rooms.

CASUAL   This style translates into "light," "simple," and "open" rooms. A sofa in a neutral-colored Haitian cotton, perhaps, some baskets on the wall, a glass-top coffee table, pastel cushions on the floor—all very comfortable and not fussy.

Don't Leave Home Without It

Take a tape measure with you everywhere while you are in the process of setting up a home. At home, make sure you measure the exterior doorframes of your apartment, and those leading to the rooms for which you are purchasing furniture (the doors can usually be taken down to move in large pieces of furniture). Measure and note space to be furnished, such as the eat-in kitchen area, so you know what will *not* work before you go shopping. Measure what you are bringing from your separate apartments or from your parents' homes, and at the store, take the dimensions of furniture before you buy. Among those who did not do this, there are many sad stories. One couple bought an elderly wicker sofa that needed some restoration work. After paying $475 for the sofa, $175 to have it spruced up, and spending another $45 for fabric to make toss pillows, they found it would not fit through the doorway of their apartment on the second floor of a two-family home. The tears that were shed over that mistake! The sofa now sits on consignment in a local antiques shop, but the couple doubt they will be able to recover their investment.

Smaller errors can be made in this area as well, such as falling in love with a coffee table that turns out to be oversized in relation to the furniture around it, or even purchasing a plant stand that is too high, or low, for the window it is meant to highlight.

If you are looking through model apartments in condominium complexes, or through new-home communities, keep in mind that furniture used in model rooms is often specially built on a smaller scale than what is sold on the open market, to give those rooms a more spacious, open feeling.

Pre-Shopping Points to Ponder

As you discuss what you need and want, the money you have to spend now and the furniture you will have to wait for, consider the following:

- Realize your limitations at the outset, and don't allow yourselves to feel "poor." Circumstances (where you are living, your careers, schooling, even your age and relative lack of earning experience) are likely to keep you from having the perfect dream of a first home. Although you may be starting out in an apartment that is not drop-dead in terms of style, and you may not love the neighborhood or the furnishings you have on hand to put into your new home, still, it can be made charming by clever use of fabric and paint and a few other suggestions that follow in the next pages. There are very few newlywed couples who have it all initially.

- Read decorating magazines. Even the most exclusive will show rooms with features or furnishings that can be adapted for those with smaller checkbook balances. Perhaps the fabric you use can be less costly than what is shown; reproductions or posters can be mounted on the walls instead of original art; restored furniture can take the place of antiques or brand-new chairs and tables. By reading these magazines you will also get a good idea of quality furnishings and what you may want to buy when you have the means or the space. The reading can be an education, helping you little by little toward the home to which you aspire.

- Before attacking expensive furniture and department stores, visit thrift stores, auctions, yard and estate sales, flea markets and used-furniture stores. Always try to see how an item might look, not how it looks now. If it looked all that good, you probably would not be finding it at these bargain-basement prices. Sad-looking wood-finish furniture can be spray-painted and perhaps stenciled, too. Lamps may need only new shades. A chipped table can be covered with a cloth or a piece of lace. Ugly pictures can be removed from attractive frames, which might need only a coat of gilt. Unusual bits of fabric can cover tabletops or can be made into cases for toss pillows. These items can be found at great savings, and the bonus is the fun of experimenting with your finds. And, of course, you will often find that the quality of the furniture at these sales, even if a piece is damaged in some minor way, is superior to what is available in stores today. If you or your husband has any talent in refinishing furniture, you can acquire tables or chairs that, with your careful attention, may become family heirlooms.

- Don't overlook the impact of paint. Pretty colors on walls can tie together a room done with hand-me-downs and make it warm and inviting. Paint can bring drama to a room sparsely furnished, or to one of no particular architectural distinction. All of the above applies to furniture, too. You wouldn't be the first to buy four unmatched wood chairs for the kitchen or dining area, and create a uniform look by painting them the same color. Or buy four nondescript matching chairs and paint each a different color. One woman created an all-white bedroom by painting a ho-hum bedstand, bookcase, and bed frame white. The walls were white, and baskets for two ficus trees were spray-painted to match. The comforter on the bed was predominantly white, with touches of leaf green. Wall art was, in the main, white, with some green and blue tones. The room was cool and elegant, with the look of a seaside house, although the sixth-floor apartment was far from the ocean.

- Try for continuity throughout your home. The eye should move from one room to another without being jarred. This means carpeting should be complementary, and so should colors. The red kitchen shouldn't be visible from the chocolate-brown dining area, which, in turn, runs into the buttercup-yellow living room. Too much. Cool it down. See the apartment as a whole, not just as individual rooms to be decorated. All of this calls for a *plan,* of course.

- Since mixing furniture styles has been "in" for years, don't be afraid to try your hand at this decorating blend. Just make sure the pieces have classic lines and the colors are coordinated. Mixing prints for slipcovers, curtains, throw pillows, and the like may be trickier for the novice than getting furniture styles to mesh, and you may have to turn to decorating magazines, or a friend with flair, or even a professional decorator (more on this below). There is a talent to creating a style and not a mishmash.

- Don't hang pictures too high on a wall, a common decorating error. Eye level could be too high. One guideline: if the bottom of a picture is one foot from the top of the sofa, that's fine.

- To see how others—besides your family and friends—live in and decorate their home, visit open houses at homes that are for sale and go on area house tours. Some excellent tips can be picked up at the latter events, and homeowners are only too happy to tell visitors where they bought the bakery rack, how they installed the chair rail and whether a neophyte do-it-yourselfer can tackle kitchen tiles.

- A charming yet very inexpensive way of decorating is with baskets. They can be arranged on a wall in place of pictures and used on the floor to store magazines or firewood. Baskets can serve as plant holders, too, and can cost far less than ceramic cachepots.

- Speaking of plants, an attractive arrangement of large plants, or just one tree, can take the place of the furniture you are not able to buy yet, and give any room instant cachet.

- You don't want to invest in costly wallpaper in a home you rent? Or don't want to bother asking the landlord's permission to paper? Try bedsheets stapled to the wall, for a warm look simulating wallpaper, yet one that is extremely cost-saving and simple to install. Bedroom sheets come in exciting patterns these days, and sheet fabric is sturdy and durable. The material is also long-lasting and large enough (using king-size sheets if necessary) to cover at least part of an average wall from ceiling to floor. If you have a sewing machine, you can sew two sheets together to cover a long wall. Or you can send the job out to your neighborhood tailor or seamstress.

  You can use a staple gun to attach the sheets right to the wall. Some home decorators use firring strips—long, narrow slats of wood—and nail them to the wall first, stapling the sheets to the strips. But many skip that extra step.

  Picture this result: a bedroom with sheets serving as wallpaper, where the comforter is made from the same fabric, with, of course, matching sheets and pillowcases. Extra sheets can be purchased for curtains, toss pillows, cushions for an easy chair, or a cloth to place over a round table. Fabric can be matching or, if that looks like too much of a good print, complementary.

- Back to wallpaper: If you do want to buy some for a room in your rental apartment, opt for strippable paper. No fuss peeling it off if you have to when you move.

- Although you may be pleased that your place has many windows, covering them all can take time and money, and matching curtains to the rest of a room may have never been your strong suit. Heavy draperies are expensive, and may not fit in your next home. In addition to making curtains from sheets, consider making them from lace material—such as tablecloths—that you have also used on tables, or upholstered pieces, or the bed. Another interesting idea is hanging plain shades, then using, as a border covering the bottom rim of the shade, material or wallpaper that matches or complements other colors in the room, skipping curtains altogether. Simpler yet, paint the bottom rim that holds the wood slat a different color. One couple eliminated all window coverings except bamboo blinds—maintenance free, attractive, and easy to install. If they have to leave them behind one day, there is no great financial loss. Note these blinds, depending on the style you buy, might be transparent. This couple lived on a high floor in their building, but you may want to keep this point in mind.

- Recessed lighting is another purchase that obviously can't be taken along if you move. If you plan to stay for a while where you are, and don't mind the financial investment (and the landlord has no objection), by all means go ahead and invest. Otherwise, opt for lamps or do-it-yourself track lights, which can be removed and taken to your next home. Your local hardware store or home decorating center can help you with materials and advice on installation.

- Expand your imagination. A quilt can be used as a tablecloth or a wall hanging, not just as a bedspread. An odd door can serve as a desk top, with a file cabinet on either side for a base. A handsome square or rectangular scarf can go into that three-dollar bargain frame. An unwanted night table can become a base for a round table for the living room. The lumber store will cut a piece of plywood to the appropriate round size for you; position it on top of the table and cover it with a cloth. Wouldn't the chair that was in your bedroom at home bring an interesting country look to the kitchen? Or how about seeing if it fits in the bathroom? Keep in mind that while an item may be sold in a particular department of a store, once you get it home it's yours to place anywhere. Some items, like stoves, have limited possibilities; on the other hand, a purchase like a black-lacquered Parsons table could have you walking around your apartment thinking for hours.

- Investigate ready-to-assemble and unpainted furniture. A few hours' work or a coat of paint or wood stain may bring you a piece that will last for years.

- Cramped for some personal, or office, space in a too-small apartment? A three-panel screen can act as a room divider, and so can bookcases and étagères.

- Also for the too-small apartment: Remember that with light colors a room seems larger; darker tones make it smaller. Don't automatically think itsy-bitsy when it comes to furnishings. A large wall painting, a sizable hutch, dramatic toss pillows instead of a grouping of small ones—all can look more attractive than dozens of small appointments.

- Get personal. The finest furniture a savings account can buy will not give your rooms the warm touch only you can create— with photographs, handmade pillows or pottery, family heirlooms, souvenirs of your travels, and treasured gifts from family and friends.

- One of the most popular decorating looks, a style that never seems to be relegated to the back of the design books, is English country. Why is this style such a staple of fabric centers, decorators' client lists, and open-house tours? Because it is homey. Fabric used in this style is often chintz, and is likely to have a few pulls in it and dog hairs here and there because animals settle in comfortably in these rooms, too. There is some sagging in the (always old) upholstered furniture. With English country, vases of fresh flowers can be found in virtually every room, and personal touches, like framed photographs, look casually arranged, but are, in fact, artfully placed. It is a comfortable look, not intimidating and not "decorated." Take a cue from that style—even if the look is not one you would want for yourself—and try not to over-decorate your own home or make it too rigidly appointed. It should encourage congenial gatherings, good conversation, and relaxed eating and drinking, or, by its comfort, make you want to sink into a chair or sofa and kick off your shoes.

Renting Furniture

If you are living in temporary quarters, are not quite sure of your buying preferences yet, or cannot afford to fill instantly the space you now have, you might consider leasing some of what you need.

Can you find style if you rent furniture?

Is the money spent actually a saving?

Let's see.

Broadly speaking, it is better to own than to rent. But if you are staying in one place only a few months or a year or so, as a result of job transfer, a military assignment, or attendance at professional school, then renting may make sense in every way.

You are in for a surprise if the last time you thought about furniture leasing you envisioned laminated furniture with plastic cushions as the only style available. The industry has upgraded its image over the last several years. Reputable companies are now carrying stock that covers all decorating styles, and many carry brand names of furniture. You can get duck cloth slipcovers and glass tabletops, French provincial sofas or contemporary sectionals. Shop rental firms the way you would look around for any other purchase, of course. Avoid those that feature junk and have exorbitantly high charges.

The companies cater to people much like yourselves—upscale transferees, military personnel, sports and show business people, travelers from overseas here for only a few months. Actor Robert Redford reportedly brought in rental furniture to his new Manhattan apartment a few years ago while his interior designer was completing work on the place. Folks who have just bought a home and do not have the money to furnish it fully, or are not sure just how they do want to furnish it, make up another market. The newly divorced are a rising sector of renters.

You will find that a rental showroom looks pretty much like the furniture section of a department store, although you are not likely to find every style and color you like. (But you won't have to wait seven months for delivery, either.) After you make a selection, a contract is written up listing those items. You may rent an entire room or individual pieces of furniture.

WORKING THE NUMBERS

Obviously, rental costs vary from one company to another and from coast to coast, but generally a three-room apartment can be furnished for as little as $50 a month or as much as $500. Costs are calculated according to each item selected. Your taste and checkbook will determine how much you spend. If you'd like to rent a sofa, you may pay $20 to $60 a month; wall units may go for $20 to $40 per section. Although basic furnishings are included in every company's inventory, many do not offer carpeting or art works. The furniture, which is sent to your home usually within forty-eight hours, can be brand-new; it has at least been cleaned and sanitized.

Most rental companies will offer you insurance. You can expect to pay a one-month deposit in advance and a delivery fee of about $50 each way. Some companies allow you to apply rental fees toward purchase.

Think about how much it would cost if you bought the furniture you want in installment payments. Yes, $300 a month in leasing fees leaves you with only rent receipts at the end of a year, while paying $300 to a department store might give you paid-for furniture after that time. But maybe you want to leave it all behind when you move on. Or you're not sure you know what you want, and might buy something that you either hate for years or give as soon as possible to the nearest Salvation Army store. Renting may be the wiser choice in this case. Perhaps you want—or need—to keep cash free for, say, your business. Then not tying it up in $15,000 worth of furniture purchases may make good financial sense.

Some words of caution, however. As mentioned earlier, some great furniture buys can be found quite cheaply by shopping around at used-furniture stores and flea markets. So don't automatically think that if you need furniture, you need new, expensive store-bought purchases. Also, just because you have purchased a seven-room house does not mean you are expected to fill up seven rooms within a month after the closing. Still, if you feel you can afford to furnish several rooms by renting, or if you have a special need to do so—perhaps you will be doing business entertaining and would like to have at least the common rooms looking good—then leasing could work out well for you.

How to find who rents: The Furniture Rental Association of America has a toll-free hotline that you can call for names of reliable firms in your area. The number is 1-800-FOR-RENT (in Ohio, call 614-895-1273).

VERY SHORT-TERM RENTALS

You might want to lease a few pieces of furniture when company comes to visit. A foldaway bed or two, for example, or folding dining chairs can be picked up easily if you need them for a special week or weekend. Your college roommate and her husband and baby are coming to town? You can rent a crib and other infant gear. These will come from rental companies listed in your Yellow Pages under Furniture Rentals which specialize in short-term leases (most furniture companies have a three-month minimum rental).

Be careful of so-called "rent-to-own" stores. Here, a portion of your rental fee is applied toward purchase after eighteen months. But by renting an appliance for that long, or not knowing its retail value, you may end up paying two, three, or more times its purchase price. For example, you might spend $1,000 for a television set or VCR costing far less than that to buy. The appeal to the consumer is in the advertised low weekly rental rates. If you decide you do need to rent from one of these places, do so for only a short time.

RENTING ART

A rather well-kept secret in the home furnishings arena is the availability of rental art. Why rent the picture over your sofa instead of buying it? For the same reasons you might want to rent furniture: you're on the move, you're not certain of your tastes, you can't afford to buy what you like. Renting art can be especially smart at this time in your lives, as you both decide what to buy in the future that will please both of you aesthetically. Maybe you were once staunch Turner enthusiasts, but now, after some gallery- and museum-hopping, you find yourselves eyeing de Kooning. You might rent modern art for a while to see if the attraction endures.

Most art museums have a lending program, and so do large public libraries. Art galleries generally do not rent, although if you are on friendly terms with the gallery owners, they may make an exception. Sometimes artists' leagues in a community will offer a rental program. Museums that do rent offer a wide and interesting variety of works, from prints to lithographs, seragraphs and oil paintings—all ready to hang right on your walls. Some are originals, while others are reproductions, handsomely framed. Sometimes there is sculpture for rent as well. You can expect to pay perhaps $30 a year to become a museum member (only members can rent art), and after that you might pay a flat fee or perhaps 10 percent of the purchase price of a particular work, although you are not required to buy. The rental period may be two months, with an option to renew for another two. A museum's rental inventory might be priced from $300 per work to $5,000, although at the Whitney Museum in New York City, by paying a $1,000 annual membership fee to the Whitney Circle, you can borrow a work of art from the museum's permanent collection for one year.

There is no security deposit required at museums, and they provide padded cases for transportation. Insurance is usually carried by the lending services, with your renter's or homeowner's policy picking up from there if further protection is needed. The purpose of these programs is strictly educational, not profit-making. The institutions' raison d'être is to initiate the novice into the huge, fascinating, and sometimes intimidating world of art. So ask all the questions you like of the museum staff. Don't be shy.

A membership card from your local public library can bring you artworks on loan at no charge at all. What is available is certainly not of museum quality, although you may be surprised. Some libraries feature only popular reproductions (like Wyeth's *Christina's World*, Bruegel's *Peasant Dance*), but others offer original works by local artists, too. At some libraries, all rental art is offered matted but unframed, and you must show either the frame you have for the work or the receipt from a frame shop if the frame is not yet ready.

Professional Decorating Help

Do you think you could use some assistance in putting together a decorating scheme? Or just use some help with colors? Maybe you are confused about furniture styles. Perhaps you don't have time to decorate at all.

So call in the professionals, from any number of sources.

Department stores with sizable furniture departments sometimes offer no-charge assistance from one of their in-house decorators for buyers making a major purchase (or two). Others charge a flat fee ($200 and up), which can be applied to purchases over a certain amount. The quality and scope of this advice will vary from one store to another, of course. But by all means ask about this service when you are making a purchase.

You might have a friend, or know of a friend of a friend, who is talented in this area and whom you might hire to decorate a room or two for you. One newly married young woman engaged her closest friend to decorate the couple's bedroom. The friend was trying to become established on a small scale in her community. She created a new look for the woman's room at a bargain rate, spray-painting old furniture that had been stored in the couple's basement. She papered the walls and shopped for a comforter, sheets, and pillows in a complementary print. Dried flowers and reeds went into miscellaneous vases and jugs, also found in the basement. In return, the woman permitted her friend to take pictures of the room and show it to two prospective clients.

How much to pay a friend? He or she may have a set fee for various decorating jobs. But if it's being done simply for friendship's sake, you may want to charge what you both think is a fair hourly rate or flat fee. Find out exactly what this friend or acquaintance will do for that fee. (Shop for furniture and fabrics? Leave the shopping to you and do only the arranging once purchases are made? The bride's friend even sewed curtains and hemmed a cloth for a table as part of her assignment. The two agreed on an hourly rate of $10 for all of the work except shopping, which they did together. The decorator waived that fee. The bill came to $140 for fourteen hours' work.)

- Another option when you need to send out an SOS is contacting a nationwide franchise like Decorating Den. Here, the decorator makes house calls, coming to your home with a van full of patterns, swatches, and paint charts. You pay for the merchandise you order—there are no design fees or delivery charge.

- You can look for an independent decorator, admittedly the most potentially expensive option. A decorator is not likely to help you with something as small as a curtain problem but will expect a more substantial assignment—like an entire room or the whole apartment or house. Some who are just starting out will take less costly jobs, however, using those assignments to fill out a portfolio.

KNOW WHAT YOU'RE SEEKING AND HOW MUCH YOU ARE WILLING TO PAY

What do you expect from this decorator? Will you give him or her carte blanche to replace items, or are there certain pieces of furniture that must stay and that the decorator must work around? Do you know exactly the style of furniture or overall look you are striving for, or are you open to suggestions? Do you have a working budget? Naturally you will not know what a decorator will charge at this point, but you can at least estimate the cost of the furniture you want to buy, the price of wallpaper, paint, lighting fixtures, carpeting, and the rest. To help the decorator, collect some pages torn from decorating magazines that feature the look you want.

DECORATING IN STAGES

You have moved into your first home, and the number of things you need seems overwhelming. What you *have* in the way of furnishings, however, is minimal. So is your budget. The smart thing to do is divide your decorating into stages. This will give you at least a comfortable—not bare—look to start, and will let you fill in and trade up as your checkbook allows, perhaps over the course of several years.

Picture your living room in these transition stages:

IN STAGE 1, the principal, most costly, purchase is a sofa. Floors remain bare. The walls are painted and window treatments are simple, perhaps only shades or blinds. The remaining furniture and accessories are what you already own, filled in with plants, baskets, and other casual touches. Large pillows or a futon on the floor takes the place of the chairs you will purchase someday. In front of the sofa is an attractive but inexpensive Parsons table.

IN STAGE 2, the living room is wallpapered. An inexpensive straw rug now covers the floor, or at least an area of it. There are more formal curtains or draperies at the windows. While you have retained some of your less costly furniture, you have also made a couple of major purchases—a wall unit, say, and an upholstered wing chair. The inexpensive prints on the walls have become more costly poster art, or perhaps some original works. An antique trunk replaces the Parsons table.

IN STAGE 3, which may be several years down the decorating road, the sofa has probably been reupholstered. Draperies are in a contrasting print or stripe. The wing chair is covered in a complementary material. The straw rug has given way to a room-size Oriental. Antique accessories have been purchased over the years, and there are a few needlepoint pillows (your handiwork?) about instead of the $9.99 polished cotton ones you started with. The room has a graceful, finished look now, one achieved after time spent carefully planning, shopping, and replacing.

FINDING THE RIGHT PERSON

You can find a decorator in any number of ways: by referral from friends; by contacting one whose work you have admired in local newspaper features, in magazines, or at designer show houses; or by calling your regional office of the American Society of Interior Designers. They can send you a questionnaire to get you started. Your answers will help ASID determine the kind of help you are seeking, and they will recommend two or three member designers in your area.

THE FEE

It will depend on what you want, and that may not necessarily be a full-scale makeover of your entire home. Some decorators will charge a flat one-day fee just for walking through your home and making suggestions for changes and telling you details on where you can purchase the furniture and materials you'll need. Some individuals will act as consultants on a long-term remodeling project, and you can call that person periodically for advice about fixtures, colors, and the like. For a more in-depth project—say, day-to-day work on several rooms—a decorator may charge a fee for the initial meeting, then ask you for your budget, and finally offer an estimate for the work. Each decorator's charge is unique, since this is a creative, subjective field. Expect little uniformity.

Billing methods vary, but since many decorators charge by the hour ($25 to $200 or more), you might ask how many hours he or she thinks the project will take. You can request that your contract read "$75 an hour, not to exceed $3,000," if that is agreed upon, so that you know there is a maximum to the fee. Other professionals charge a percentage of the total job, which can run from 15 to 35 percent. If the work comes to $10,000 and the decorator's fee is 20 percent, you will be billed $2,000. A few charge by the square foot, perhaps $25 to $50 per square foot.

Get *everything* in writing. The decorator's contract should spell out the scope of the project, setting forth the extent of both the decorator's responsibilities and yours (maybe you are to do the painting or some other aspect of the job). Starting and completion dates should be written down. The contract should also contain detailed information about fees and how billing is to be handled. After evaluating professional assistance, spend some time talking over these points:

- Did the references of the designer you liked check out?

- Can you do some of this work yourselves, saving money, if not time?

- What about your priorities? Can one of these projects be put on the back burner while you rethink what you want or wait to come up with more money?

- Finally, and perhaps most important, remember this is *your* home. You do not have to have a decorator's taste thrust upon you. It's a partnership, not poor little you trembling before an intimidating man or woman turning up a nose at everything you possess or hope to accomplish.

It's hard work, attempting to furnish a first home. You are probably trying to achieve a blending of two quite independent (we will not say stubborn) tastes, working with a budget that is not all that lavish, and a panicky sense of "What do I do first?" and "*Now* what do I do?" The day will come, of course, when the work will be over and you will mercifully settle into the comfort it has brought, when the near-disasters, tears, and frantic shopping, and, yes, even the quarrels over who has the taste in the family, will fade. Guests will compliment you on your home. You will compliment yourselves. It's done—or at least as much as any home is ever "done." Relax and enjoy it!

HOW COMPATIBLE ARE YOUR TASTES?

Just for fun, and perhaps for some insight into how each of you approaches decorating, see how you fare with this brief quiz.

	YOU	HIM
My favorite color schemes are		
bright primary colors		
smoky colors—grays, roses, mauves		
startling blacks, whites, reds		
a monochromatic look		
other:		
The living-room style I prefer is		
contemporary		
traditional		
eclectic		
romantic		
dramatic		
country		
casual		
For the floors, I like		
wall-to-wall carpeting		
bare wood, with a few scatter rugs		

	YOU	HIM
stenciled floors		
other:		
I think a television set belongs in		
the living room		
the bedroom		
other:		
To me, windows look most attractive when covered with		
formal draperies		
sheer curtains		
blinds (venetian, bamboo)		
shutters		
just window shades		
a mix of the above, depending on the room and its decor		
Which is you?		
I would rather buy inexpensively so that the apartment quickly looks completed.		

	YOU	HIM
I prefer waiting for just the right piece, and don't mind a somewhat bare look in the meantime.		
The stereo system we have now is		
A-one		
just adequate		
We need a new one—let's shop.		
Some decorators say that a bedroom should reflect a woman's taste.		
I agree.		
No, the room should be a blend of the couple's tastes.		
Work or hobby space for us in our home is		
crucial		
nice, but not necessary		
unimportant		
Narrowing things down a little:		
We need more		

	YOU	HIM
The one thing she/he's bringing to our new home that I detest is		
If I were handed a check for $1,000 and told it had to be spent on something for the home, I would buy		
All our computer gear should be placed in		
I think we should acquire furniture by (waiting until we can afford each piece/ using credit cards/borrowing to buy)		

5

STORAGE: GETTING THE MOST SPACE FROM YOUR PLACE

An apartment fills up quickly, doesn't it? There is a little of your stuff here, a little of his there, plus a few new purchases. There are boxes of books, deck furniture from your former place (a definite can't-use in your new high-rise), some furniture odds and ends, plus all the gear you would like to store just from one season to the next—ski equipment, golf clubs, beach umbrella and chairs. You don't want to get rid of all this permanently (the furniture can be used in the home you will have one day), but there is no room for it in your four rooms and bath, either.

Your folks have just announced they are selling the homestead and moving to a condominium in Arizona. And here is a news bulletin: would you please *do* something about everything you have stored in the basement from childhood and, by the way, would you like to take your old bedroom suite?

What do you do with such an embarrassment of riches—yours, his, wedding gifts, recent joint purchases? Obviously, this is a problem mainly for apartment dwellers, although if you already own a home you may pick up a tip or two as well. Even in houses, space can be tight.

Which is interesting—and curious. Construction of new houses and apartments has brought less storage space over the years, even as Amercians have become more acquisitive. This has been the trend since after World War II, when Americans started on the path to becoming super-consumers. Cathedral ceilings, while certainly attractive, take up space that could be given over to storage. Other features of new homes, such as open, undefined areas, circular stairways, carports, and the absence of attics also leave buyers with fewer square feet in which to store their new purchases, and their old ones. So the richer we become, the more we are able to buy—and the more costly our apartments and houses become—the less space we are actually being offered in which to store these possessions.

A few builders have heard the call for a need for storage space and are reinstituting the pantry, which, in fact, is often taken out of older homes when the new owners remodel, in order to make the kitchen larger. Builders are also constructing larger garages, which can accommodate some of a family's gear. Landlords occasionally provide storage space in a basement, but that is frequently only a locker or an unsecured corner, prey to theft and mildew.

If you were living in separate quarters before your marriage, you can see quickly that you cannot put everything from your three rooms and his two rooms into a four-room apartment. There is one room too few, and that's not counting the wedding gifts, and cleaning out the folks' basement and all the new furnishings you will be buying together. What you should be doing at this stage is deciding what you will take to your new home and what will go into storage. Perhaps you will have another option. Maybe *his* folks are not moving to Arizona and will allow you to keep a few things in their basement, if they have one. This is only a temporary measure, however. Parents of grown children may not want more "stuff" in their basements and attics. Parents of grown children may be into their own weeding-out process.

Stephanie Culp, a professional organizer in Los Angeles, advises that you each do your own preliminary sorting of your current apartment, and then consult each other on what you plan to bring to your new home. She adds that what each of you decides to bring should *not* be a surprise to the other on moving day.

Culp points out that the biggest problem when two people bring two households together is duplication. Even a man who isn't terribly domestic, she says, is likely to bring a spatula. And you have a spatula. There are often duplications in wedding gifts, too. If you're not likely to need more than one of an item— you may have received five sets of crystal wineglasses—the extras should be returned.

Not everyone's winnowing-out endeavor is perfect, of course. Says Jody, who has been married one year and is living with her husband, Dan, in a three-and-a-half-room condo: "We both had our own apartments before we married, so you'd think we'd keep the newer toaster and blender and microwave and iron, etcetera, and get rid of the older one. But I kept thinking, Newer isn't *brand*-new. What if the one we save dies soon? So I insisted we keep all the duplicates, too. Dan said he didn't care since it's in storage and he doesn't have to look at it.

"I feel we'll save money someday by doing this, but I'll tell you I also feel like I have this massive appliance monkey on my back. You know how many appliances the average household has? Now we have two, and in some cases three, of every one of them!"

Storage space—besides the folks' basement—can be found in the basements of some rental buildings, in garages, basements, and toolsheds of apartments in some private homes, and in many condominiums' special storage rooms (these are small, and a unit-owner gets only one of them). If you can take advantage of these extra square feet, congratulations. If you have nothing but the space inside your own four walls, consider this. . . .

The Self-Storage Solution

You may have seen these structures along major highways, where they tend to be new, sprawling one-story buildings. Sometimes a banner is waving in the breeze created by the traffic: "Self-Storage: Inquire Within." In town, they are more likely to be converted warehouse buildings.

Self-storage became popular about a decade ago, when at first the buildings were called mini-warehouses. In a mobile society, with smaller households, the growth of single-parent families, divorced folks and never-married people living on their own, it fills a need that allows pack rats to hold on to every little item, even if they live in apartments the size of Diamond matchboxes.

It works like this: Cubicles, which generally start at five feet by five feet, and may be as large as room size, are available for rent on a short-term basis, from a few months to a few years. The cost for the smallest space is as little as $10 a month in some parts of the country; the larger units can cost as much as several hundred dollars. In the main, they are still less costly, and more accessible, than traditional warehouses used for storage of household goods. In fact, with the suburban one-story self-storage spaces, you can drive your car right up to your unit, for easy loading and unloading.

Some mini-units are climate controlled, and some have electrical outlets, so more than one has served as someone's "office" or practice studio, in addition to being a storage space. You can find those closest to you by checking the Yellow Pages under Storage or Warehouses. Most self-storage companies have an on-site manager who can answer your questions.

A mini can be great for storing out-of-season sports equipment, old files, furniture you have no particular use for now, inherited odds and ends you'll *never* have any use for but wouldn't dream of pitching out. And things like the table you'll refinish one of these days, the tea service you'll use when you're a lady of leisure, the crib you just inherited but don't plan on using for a long, long time.

Karen is a young woman, although no longer a newlywed, who uses the mini-storage unit she and her husband, Ben, rent to store, in addition to other items, the wreaths she makes and sells on consignment to boutiques in the area. Some are made of ribbons, others of branches, dried flowers, and baby's breath; they all need room to breathe so that their ingredients will not get mashed or crumble and fall apart. There is no room in their apartment, so Karen spreads them out in the storage unit until she has enough for the next shipment. "They're on top of boxes and bureaus and all over the place there," she says, "but after all, a warehouse doesn't have to be *decorated,* so I really don't care how it looks. I've got my space."

When choosing a mini, consider the following:

- Talk to the manager to see what size you need, and know in advance exactly how much gear you plan to stow.

- Make sure the location and hours are convenient for you. Some are open around-the-clock; others have set visiting hours.

- Is the building well maintained? Check for obvious water marks on the ceiling or walls, which indicate leaks.

- Are pickup and delivery services available?

- Read the contract carefully for information on payments, deposits, access to the unit, and *what happens to the goods if you skip a payment.*

- Ask the manager about *their* insurance coverage, and then check with *your* insurance agent to round out the insurance picture.

- Be sure to ask what is *not* permitted in a storage unit—food, for example, and certain items that may not fare well, given the year-round temperature setting of the building. (Ask this before you store woolens and furs there for the summer.)

- Is the neighborhood safe and well lit at night, so you do not have to worry about going there in the evening by yourself?

GREAT STORAGE AIDS

- A lazy susan, in any cabinet or closet, or even the refrigerator, to make all stored items accessible

- Wall units

- Professionally organized, and possibly rebuilt, closets

- Pantries (the pieces of furniture—the rooms are usually found these days only in higher-priced new homes)

- An undersink rack/rollout wire basket

- A ceiling pot/pan rack

- Built-in storage space under a window seat or stairway

- A garage or toolshed

- A cubicle away from home in a self-storage warehouse

Taking a Look at Your Apartment

Once items not immediately needed are stored somewhere outside your apartment, you can concentrate on what's going to go into your home. Think it might not all fit? Here are some points to consider:

- If you haven't already selected your apartment, it goes without saying that storage space—or potential space (high ceilings, unbroken wall space)—should be a factor in your decision. If you're hunting in multifamily buildings, don't forget to ask about stowing your belongings in a basement or other area used by tenants. Many would-be renters pitch things they would rather keep, only to find later that storage space is available.

- Before moving in, try to divide possessions not being used immediately into "dead storage" and "present storage." The "dead" items go into the farthest reaches of closets or into a storage bin in the basement. "Present storage," which might include extra blankets for guests and other occasionally used items, can go under the bed or in similar, more accessible spots.

- The furniture you buy now can help keep furnishings, clothing, and other items out of sight but still within your four walls. Consider, for example, a bed with storage drawers beneath. Or an armoire where audio and video equipment can be hidden from sight and will not take up valuable shelf or wall space. A sleeper sofa can accommodate guests. A living-room coffee table becomes a dining table, either by itself or by placing a piece of plywood over it to make it larger, and covering all with a cloth. This is for casual, sitting-on-the-floor meals, of course. Other kinds of tables can also give you more room. Consider drop-leaf and flip-top models that take up little space when placed against a wall, yet can expand admirably for dining, games, office work, and other uses.

- Is there a corner of a hallway that's not being used? Try finding a chest of drawers or a trunk that fits into that cranny. It can be painted, or stained, draped with a cloth or a bit of lace and become part of the hallway decor. No one will know it's storing blankets and quilts.

Once You're In

Does it look pretty crowded? Now is the time to make use of every inch of space in your place. The potential of some storage spots may be obvious, the potential of others less readily apparent. By considering storage as you move in, you can save yourselves from tossing out items you'd really like to keep if you had the room. You can also save yourselves from feeling needlessly cramped because too much is in view and not relegated to an out-of-sight storage spot. A point to consider here, of course, is whether you want to invest the money and time in built-in projects in a place that is not yours. Will the landlord allow you to build them, for that matter? And without raising the rent? (There's more about this issue in Chapter 3.)

If you do decide to make whatever changes are necessary to live there more comfortably for the next year (or three or five)—and at least give the illusion of space—here are more suggestions.

KITCHEN

No need to describe the size of the typical apartment kitchen—and the typical appliances busy people want in that room these days. Where to put all those whirring, shaking, popping gadgets? You can try for more space by mounting such small appliances as a toaster or a blender on shelves you can hang for that purpose. Is there a little space around the refrigerator where you can build cabinets? Space between the refrigerator and, say, the stove where you can construct a small, narrow closet for brooms and an ironing board?

Don't miss a spot in the kitchen. If after you put up shelves there's still room to add more storage space, hang pegboards to which you can attach pans, molds, potholders and the like. Hang a pot rack from the ceiling. You might also be able to install a simple rack or two on the inside of cabinet doors, for storing spices, wooden spoons, plastic wrap, or other items needed often. Too many pots and pans? Stash some of them in the oven, an old strategy dating back to the first tenant who lived in a cramped studio apartment.

Finally, look to Rubbermaid, producers of all kinds of expanded shelving, freestanding drawers, and lazy susans. Some of these items can help organize, condense, and make more accessible the dozens of groceries and gadgets packed into a typical tiny apartment kitchen.

LIVING-DINING AREA

Do you have a staircase where you can add storage space by cutting into the empty area at its foot to create a closet? Is there a bay window? Try making the space in front of it into storage cabinets, with the top serving either as a wooden (or choose another surface) window seat or a ledge for displaying plants or collectibles. You can store china, silver, and linen in that cabinet. The cost will depend on the space and material you prefer, but $50 to $100 worth of plywood could do the job.

Cathedral ceilings, a popular trend in new housing, nowadays, also take up valuable space that can be put to storage use. Try built-in shelving all the way up to the ceiling, using rolling library ladders to gain access to the top shelves.

Wall units, whether simple shelving nailed to the wall or a freestanding piece of furniture, have been the salvation of more than one apartment dweller. When planning a shopping expedition for them, first decide: Are you going to use the units for books and bric-a-brac? Or for record albums, videotapes, stereo speakers, the television and VCR too? Try to avoid *too* many different kinds of items on wall units, or the effect will be cluttered—just what you're trying to avoid.

Before you go shopping, measure what you plan to store in the unit. You might want to use a yardstick to get the height, width, and depth of the television set, or the stereo, or some other bulky object you want, to make sure it fits. For books and bric-a-brac, you can measure just the length of what you have on display now, allowing another one third for empty space, for items you want to bring out of boxes, and for new purchases, either now or a little down the road. You probably won't get a definitive "We need exactly thirty-five feet of shelving," but you will have a very handy ballpark figure, which can save you a trip back to the store for more materials.

LOFT

Not a room, certainly, but a space that can be created in the living area or a bedroom. This might also be a solution to your space-starved apartment, whether you build it yourself or call in a carpenter. Loft space can be the size of a bed or can be spacious enough to accommodate a few other pieces of furniture. Access is by ladder, of course. Jeanne and Lew constructed a loft above their living area just large enough for a sleeper sofa for guests and a desk and file cabinet for Lew, a full-time teacher and part-time writer. Files are not particularly attractive, so the two ran a row of low plants along the railing that defined the loft space, to hide the clutter behind it. The landlord gave them carte blanche for the installation and paid for the construction materials.

"We love this apartment," Jeanne says. "We know we'll be here for a while, so we wanted to do this. We also installed barnwood siding and cabinets in the kitchen. Sal, our landlord, knows we're improving his property, so he lets us go ahead with our plans. And all it's taking is time, really, not money on our part."

BATHROOM

These rooms usually offer at least a small patch of wall space where an open shelf can be installed, adding to the minuscule space of a medicine chest. Roomier baths allow for chests for storage or étagères for towels, guest soaps, and the like.

BEDROOM

Here is where most of us expect space, in closets that often disappoint. Walk-ins are not that common in apartments, and sliding-door closets almost always mean the area in the middle becomes the Wardrobe Bermuda Triangle—hang clothes there and you never see them again! If you're faced with one of these closets, try replacing the doors with louvers that open out.

Closet organizers—the people—have cropped up in sizable numbers over the last half-dozen years or so. For a flat fee or an hourly rate, an organizer will come to your apartment, take a look at your closet space and all that you expect to be able to store there (they will not shriek!), take some measurements, and return a few days or weeks later with material to reconstruct that space for maximum use and accessibility. The initial consultation can be free; closet reconstruction, depending on cost of materials, built-in cabinetry, etc., can run several hundred dollars. One woman gave her son and daughter-in-law a visit from a custom closet organizer as one of her wedding gifts.

Closet organizers—the materials—can be purchased at home centers and lumberyards. Closet Maid organizing kits, one example, provide shelving, baskets, and hardware. Even purchases of plastic boxes, stackable or wire racks, and shoe bags—available at the five-and-ten—can help you put your closets together with a minimal investment of time and money.

Stephanie Culp offers a Golden Rule to every couple, guaranteed to keep clutter pared down in even the smallest quarters: "If something new comes in, something old goes out. If you buy new glasses, get rid of the old Burger King glasses. Don't just put the new ones on a high shelf to be admired and not used. . . . All you have is more things that are stored."

6

SO WHO DOES THE HOUSEWORK?

The oven hasn't been cleaned in . . . how long has it been now? You can write "Dust Me" on some furniture, and indeed someone has (was it your husband, or, worse, a guest?). The kitchen floor needs a scrubbing, and the list goes on and on. But you're both busy, and what free time you do have, you're certainly not going to spend buffing and scouring.

Or perhaps there is a different scenario at your place. One of you, the other believes, is too intense about cleaning. Indeed, neurotic. The other one, *that* spouse holds, is far too laid back on the subject. Not only doesn't mind dirt, doesn't even see it.

If one of these descriptions sounds like life in your home, even in these early days of marriage, you are not alone. Surveys on the subject of housework have been conducted by several national groups over the last few years, and the results show that Americans nowadays are cleaning less and buying fewer cleaning products. Analysts say the American home is dirtier now than at any time in the last four decades!

Why this evolution toward griminess? New attitudes about cleanliness and a more relaxed population not given to scrubbing and mopping, for one thing. Smaller household size, with fewer occupants to pitch in and do the polishing and spraying, for another. But the major factor is—you guessed it—more and more women taking jobs outside the home, and they just plain have less time to spend cleaning it.

Professor Ruth Cowan, director of women's studies and a professor of history at the State University of New York at Stony Brook, Long Island, is the author of "More Work for Mother," a sociological history of women's work in the home, which appeared in a 1987 issue of *American Heritage.* She says that even a generation ago houses were "compulsively clean," but times have certainly changed.

Professor Cowan reports: "Twenty-five or thirty years ago the standards of house cleanliness were really bizarre. There was this notion that your floor had to be so clean that you could eat off it. Well, that's ridiculous—we don't eat off floors."

Changing lifestyles and demands, and a shifting focus of attention, now allow all of us the luxury of unpolished linoleum. Still, there is a modicum of cleaning that must be done in any household to keep marital sanity—and prevent a visit from the local Board of Health.

A laid-back approach is fine, if you both agree. But what if *you* prefer a spotless household? Do you mind the fact that you get no support from your husband? Would you rather do the chores yourself to be sure they are done "properly"? Does he pitch in in other areas of household maintenance, so that you do not feel unfairly burdened? Or what if *he's* the one endlessly straightening up? Does he make you feel guilty, not to mention slatternly? Or do you give him free rein to clean to his heart's delight, without a twinge of guilt?

Cleaning doesn't bother Ellen at all—because she lets her husband, Jim, do most of it. Ellen spends a good deal of her time at home in front of a computer with work she has brought from the office. Jim is bothered by a messy apartment and she isn't. But is there another subtlety at play here? Ellen earns perhaps $5,000 to $7,000 more a year than Jim. Could that make Jim feel he has to pitch in more than his share? She doubts it:

"If Jim hated cleaning and then turned around and did more than he does now, I'd say maybe he felt that was one way to contribute more to the marriage. But he truly is a neatness fanatic—his whole family is. And I'm almost oblivious to how the place looks. I love my home, and Jim and I spent a lot of time decorating it. But once it's done, I guess I'm not that much into upkeep."

Wives are not automatically the keepers of the cleaning products shrine, and husbands are not always the ones who leave a trail of mess and clutter. If you take a poll among your friends, you'll likely find just as many women as men who do not care all that much about having the cleanest place in town. And an equal number who leap up and start emptying ashtrays before the guests leave.

A Predisposition to Clean—or Not

Maybe there is something more to "wanting to clean" than simply a compulsion that grew out of one's upbringing, or the lasting effects of an either messy or obsessive college roommate. Much of one's behavior is determined by which side of the brain is dominant. Two psychologists have suggested that "left-brain" persons, who are likely to be logical and structured, are more apt to be interested in dusting and cleaning. Those more likely to be sloppy are "right-brain" persons, who tend to be creative and intuitive.

Selwyn Mills and Max Weisser are therapists who looked into the subject of how these two types can cohabit without murder being committed. For their book *The Odd Couple,* the two randomly surveyed a thousand people on the real-life conflicts that can ensue when a Oscar Madison type teams up with a Felix Unger. They discovered that the sloppy-neat match-up occurred in eighty percent of the people surveyed.

The authors recognize the difficulties involved when opposite types who are attracted to each other become annoyed when their differences inevitably surface. This would be around the time one starts screaming, "Why can't you pick up your clothes? Do you think I'm your mother? I can't stand this mess!" And the other grumbles, "Why do you have to be so uptight? Loosen up a little. How can you enjoy life with that rigid attitude?" The authors offer no solution beyond identifying the problem and suggesting that those who have it try to work around it, as befits sensible people.

Obviously, the best pairing is couples who fall midway between the two extremes. If serious differences do occur, a compromise can be reached by talking about the issue, and you may need to constantly remind each other of any resolutions you both have made. Some couples never do compromise. One simply throws up his or her hands and lets haphazard cleaning or eat-off-the-floor neatness prevail. And yes, over the years sometimes unspoken resentment about the issue takes the place of the initial anger, or perhaps good humor.

We Can Work It Out

It is difficult for most women to turn away completely from cleaning, even if their careers force them to work sixty-hour weeks. If they have not been brought up by neat-as-a-pin mothers, they still have been exposed to outside forces that ask tartly, "What kind of woman keeps a dirty home?" Yet career women receive another message, through advertising, that time spent cleaning is a throwback to pre-liberation days, and no one appreciates a housewife's agonizing over fabric softeners and floor wax. Women are sent conflicting signals—that obsession with dirt is not "in," and that they should still have homes as tidy as their mother's, even though Mom may not have held an outside job. How can *you* handle this conflict? By talking to your spouse to decide on a work schedule that is balanced for the both of you. This may mean that he does all the cleaning and you do the cooking. Or that he handles the heavy cleaning and you take on the lighter chores. Or that he does the tasks he doesn't find repugnant, like the laundry, while you do those *you* can face, like ironing, which you have always enjoyed. The rest you split. Jobs that you both loathe—washing the venetian blinds, for example—you alternate. (Or you can *pay* the other to do the job when your turn comes around!)

Any accommodation can be made. Like so many other aspects of life and relationships these days, who does the cleaning is open to negotiation to new rules. What works for you is what matters, no matter how offbeat the system may seem to relatives and friends. When you come to think of it, do you really know anyone who cares whether it's you or your husband who bundles up the newspapers for recycling?

Perhaps you are not two full-time working people. Maybe he is a student, working, for the most part, at home on an advanced degree. Or maybe you work part-time and he has a full-time job. Then chores can be balanced a little so that the one putting in a forty-hour workweek doesn't feel unfairly burdened.

One sobering thought, however: no matter how considerate your husband is and no matter how many hours *you* work, it will most likely be you who, even if you don't do all the work, will at least be "responsible" for it. That is to say, your husband may "help," but will have to be told or reminded what to do and will rarely take the initiative when it comes to actually doing the chores. This has been proven in several studies in recent years. Women do, on the average, 80 to 90 percent of household chores, even when they hold outside jobs. Men still expect their wives to do most of the cooking and the food shopping, for example. In fact, the studies add, many men find housework, as a whole, demeaning.

There are those who would say "train him right, right from the start," and indeed many young couples these days do have a more equitable division of labor than their parents did. Sometimes this comes about after intense discussion and—let's be honest—intense fighting. Often, dividing the work is relatively easy when a woman has married a man who grew up doing chores and maintaining an apartment, one who has no stereotypical ideas of how marriage works as far as housework goes. But a sizable majority of men—and even some women—do hold to traditional roles. In these unions, the "wife-does-this-and-the-husband-does-that" style of living becomes even more pronounced as years pass and children appear on the scene.

Don't try to be Superwoman, either because it's easier to do it all than to make waves or because you still feel most of the tasks around the house are "woman's work." You have married, it is assumed, a reasonable and kind man. Talk about an equitable assignment of duties, and that doesn't have to mean a 50-50 split. (Indeed, as the surveys suggest, you are not likely to be "helped" as much as you would like.) Just so you both feel the scales are reasonably well balanced. That's only fair.

Keeping Chores to a Minimum

Here are some tips from the trenches, ideas to help you organize cleaning and, even better, one or two brilliant suggestions that may make some of it absolutely unnecessary.

- Dust before you vacuum. Dust from top to bottom, and the top includes the tops of door frames, valances, and ceiling fixtures. Those should be attacked once a month. Furniture and everything else dust falls on—once a week.

- You will have a lot less to clean if you throw away junk, clear clutter, and if you toss or give away duplicates of what each of you brings from your previous households. Don't miss a lobby or block sale—not to buy, but to sell a year's worth of accumulations, which can often fill a table.

- If you keep windows clean, the bathroom sparkling, and newspapers, soda cans, and the like cleaned up, your place will look all right if company drops in suddenly. It will look neat, which subconsciously sends an "it's clean, too" message.

- Perhaps this is obvious, but: if you want your husband to help with some specific chore, *ask* him.

- A comforter is less work than a bedspread. The comforter serves as a blanket, and is just pulled down in the evening and up in the morning. No need for hospital corners!

- Wicker, a general term that applies to rattan, bamboo, and anything woven, is easier to maintain than polished woods. Dust falls on wicker, but you can't see it and you certainly can't write your name in it. A little washing down now and then constitutes upkeep.

- Ask your landlord if you can install a washer/dryer in your unit (space permitting, of course). Very time-saving.

- Covering something with something else makes two items to wash or clean. Consider dining: a round tablecloth to the floor, for example, with a smaller cloth on top of it, and fabric placemats on top of that makes three layers of laundry. The same goes for area rugs on top of wall-to-wall carpeting.

- Small houseplants—windowsill size—make for more work (vacuuming dead leaves from the floor, watering, feeding, sprinkling). Unless you are truly into greenery, why not go with a few large ones, or even potted trees, for a dramatic statement?

- Jim, who does most of the cleaning for Ellen and himself, put up bamboo blinds, eliminating the curtains they had previously installed. Those blinds—or matchsticks—unlike even venetian blinds, are almost maintenance-free, requiring only occasional dusting. Curtains and draperies are on the high end of the upkeep scale. If you prefer curtains in, say, the living room, you can still opt for no-work blinds in other areas.

- Learn from this: Taking the easy way out in landscaping turned into disaster for Nancy and Pete, who began married life in a city brownstone. Their yard was minuscule, of course. They planted small bushes around the edges, and then Pete dumped pounds and pounds of tiny pebbles in the center. The yard turned into the largest cat litter box in town! Now the yard is fieldstone.

- Don't be tense about a little disarray. It makes a home look lived in.

Hiring Help

Another solution, of course, to the battle of the dustballs is to hire someone to do it all—or at least a sizable chunk of it. If you are both working, it's likely you will be able to manage at least some help.

First, decide exactly what work you want done. Does periodic heavy cleaning get you down? Do you want someone to handle surface cleaning once a week—say, mopping the kitchen floor, cleaning the bathroom, and dusting? What about windows?

Depending on where you live, you have several options for finding Ms. or Mr. Clean. You can investigate a domestic employment agency; you can sign up with a large, franchise cleaning operation—Merry Maids, Inc., and Maid Brigade, for example, are nationwide franchises—or you can find a local one- or two-person outfit. You can also look for one individual by advertising in the help-wanted section or, better yet, by asking friends.

According to the U.S. Commerce Department, the number of franchisers providing housecleaning or maid services is growing rapidly, which is attributable, for the most part, to two-career families. Women may love having a clean house, but they hate to spend time cleaning it.

When looking for household help, keep the following in mind:

- Don't let anyone make you feel guilty about hiring help to clean your one-bedroom apartment. If you do not have the time or the inclination to clean, then why not let someone else do it? Simple.

- In talking to a domestic help agency, be sure the interviewer knows exactly what you will be asking of an employee. Make a list for yourself of what you want done. Don't keep adding new chores with each applicant you interview or forgetting some from one person to the next.

- Agencies are set up in different ways. Some supply one permanent worker, for whom you pay a fee, as you would with any employment agency. Others work like temporary agencies, only here the "temp" will clean instead of type. You will be charged an hourly rate, a percentage of which the agency keeps, while passing on the rest to the worker. If you don't like the person who comes one week, you can ask for someone different the next.

- Beware of political sensibilities in hiring. Black women may be pressured by black friends if they engage black help. White women may feel they will be perceived as insensitive for hiring a minority person. If an applicant wants the job and is qualified, and you want to pay for a service, then go ahead. This is a business from which both sides stand to profit.

- When you interview potential help, look for enthusiasm from them, and convey to them that this is an important job to you and you expect good work. Do this pleasantly, of course, not sternly. There are still people who enjoy working for someone who appreciates their efforts.

- Does the applicant present a neat, clean appearance? Sloppy candidates for the job are not likely to be industrious about cleaning your home.

- Be sure interviewees know what cleaning supplies you have. Will you have to buy more? Will the cleaning person bring his or her own? Ask about flexibility—will the applicant be able to help out with parties? for example. If you settle this issue early on, you'll save yourself the disappointment or annoyance of being turned down when you ask a few months after they are hired.

- Where does this applicant live? How will he or she get to your place? Do you pay for carfare?

- Check references, an absolutely essential step in hiring. This person will, after all, have access to your home.

- If you are hiring someone permanently, ask the agent about the applicant's job performance, of course, but also why he or she is looking for a new position. How efficient was the worker on his or her last job? Is the applicant punctual? Dependable? Trustworthy? A self-starter?

- Can't find anyone willing to do windows? You may have to engage a window-cleaning agency for that chore. Some handle only commercial and industrial clients, but there are still a few who will take on residential cleaning.

- In the same vein, if you want other special jobs done, you may be able to find workers where you live. There are gofers who can run errands, for instance, some of whom have turned their services into trendy, money-making enterprises. Someone to do your grocery shopping is another possibility. And so, of course, are pet services and services offering minor household repairs. There may be individuals in your town who will hire themselves out to balance your checkbook, pack for a move, and do anything else you want done. You can find a specialist who will accompany you on a buying trip for a specific item, like an automobile or video equipment. Help is everywhere—for a price, of course.

Having someone else do the cleaning will generally cost you $35 to $55 a week. That's for cleaning one day. You may decide that having a worker in for a day every other week is enough for you and your budget.

It will probably come as no surprise to you, since it may take some time to find a good housecleaning person, that a jewel should be treated like one, or he or she will move on to a more appreciative household. If good help is scarce, don't quibble over the small stuff. By all means be lavish with praise for work well done. (You like a pat on the back when *you're* doing a good job, don't you?) Offer a day or two of vacation pay each year, and a Christmas gift of a day's wages. Employers usually do not pay a once-a-week cleaning person who calls in sick.

Talk with your helper often, to make sure instructions are being understood and followed, and to keep the lines of communication open. Don't be too fussy. No one, or almost no one, is likely to clean perfectly, but your instructions should be followed. How you prefer having towels folded, for instance, is a small point, but having that chore done the way you want is a reasonable expectation. You may have to show a worker how you want things done, instead of merely telling him or her.

What if it isn't working out? If you have honestly made an effort with the helper, to no avail, fire him or her quickly. Do not agonize or put it off. This is a business arrangement and requires a professional decision. Two weeks' notice is usual, but if the situation is very uncomfortable, the dismissal may take effect immediately.

There is bound to be some disappointment, or a problem or two, in hiring outside help. But those annoyances can seem minor when compared with trying to do every household chore personally in spite of a hectic work schedule. You are buying time for yourself, time to spend on more valuable and enjoyable pursuits. You deserve it.

SO HOW DO YOU FEEL ABOUT DIRT?

	YOU	HIM
I think housework can easily be done in _____ hours a week.		
Housework:		
It should be evenly divided between us.		
The one who puts in the longer work hours should do less.		
Men should do the heavy chores, women the everyday upkeep.		
We'll have to adapt almost every chore and who does it to our own situation.		
I prefer cleaning		
in the morning		
after work		
on weekends		
I can stand		
dirt more than clutter		
clutter over dirt		
I particularly can't stand a dirty (kitchen/bathroom, etc.)		
The mess he/she makes that really annoys me is		

	YOU	HIM
The cleaning job I most detest is		
The one I find least odious is		
The one gadget/appliance we couldn't do without is		
Next, I think we should buy		
I think his/her overall approach to house-work is		
too compulsive for me		
too laid back for me		
sudden shifts from one to the other		
can't determine a pattern		
fine with me, whatever it is		

WHO DOES WHAT?

Here is a worksheet that might help you split chores, so that neither of you is stuck with too many dreadful ones. A fair division of labor should emerge—or at least one tolerable to you both.

		CAN TOLERATE	ALMOST ENJOY	DETEST	LET'S HIRE OUT
Vacuuming	YOU				
	HIM				
Washing windows	YOU				
	HIM				
Dusting/polishing	YOU				
	HIM				
Cleaning bathroom and kitchen	YOU				
	HIM				
Laundry	YOU				
	HIM				
Ironing	YOU				
	HIM				
Oven cleaning	YOU				
	HIM				
Food shopping	YOU				
	HIM				

		CAN TOLERATE	ALMOST ENJOY	DETEST	LET'S HIRE OUT
Pet care	YOU				
	HIM				
Minor repairs	YOU				
	HIM				
Doing dishes	YOU				
	HIM				
Minor painting	YOU				
	HIM				
Lawn/yard work	YOU				
	HIM				
Trash/newspapers	YOU				
	HIM				
Drop off/pick up at dry cleaners	YOU				
	HIM				
Plant care	YOU				
	HIM				

7

SHOULD YOU LIVE WITH YOUR FOLKS (or His) TO SAVE FOR A HOME?

Lori and Bill lived with his parents for a little over a year after their marriage. The arrangement worked—for the most part.

"We all got along well," says Lori, a twenty-four-year-old paralegal. "But maybe that's because everyone was very considerate, very polite, and really didn't want arguments or any dissension. All that niceness could be a strain sometimes, though, since my temperament is more like 'Speak up! Get it off your chest!' "

Lori explains that she and her husband, who has his own small printing company, wanted to buy a home eventually, and realized they could save more quickly if they didn't have to pay open-market rent.

Luckily, Bill's parents had extra room in their suburban home, a large Victorian clapboard, and wanted to do their part to help their son and daughter-in-law. So they offered to share their home with the younger couple. Lori and Bill paid them $200 a month, almost a token amount for that community.

At the time of their marriage, both had been living in their own apartments, with roommates. Bill was paying $400 a month, Lori and the two women with whom she shared an apartment each paid $275. The couple's combined savings was $6,000, but they anticipated a hike in that figure after the wedding. They weren't disappointed. Their wedding gifts—in cash and checks—came to $3,000.

Still, they felt $9,000 was too little to begin the househunt, and both very much wanted their own place. All that room at Bill's folks seemed alluring, so they decided to move in. Once they had saved enough to enable them to go out with $15,000 or $20,000, they reasoned, they would leave. Even that, Lori felt, was certainly not a lot these days. Still, it would buy them a starter condominium in an attractive new complex in one of the many suburbs that surrounded the city where they both worked. She liked both his parents, although since she and Bill had lived and dated in the city, there had not been all that much contact with them. Her own parents were seventeen hundred miles away. Lori now says she just took a deep breath, thought of the money to be saved, and plunged into her lifestyle. "I thought I might have to make nice a lot," she recalls, "and I really had the sense that having it work was going to be up to me, but I assumed I could do it. Bill was close to his folks, there were no bad feelings there, so I sort of thought positive."

When both generations are willing to sacrifice some privacy and adapt themselves to what will probably be somewhat cramped quarters, moving in with the folks for a while makes good financial sense. And an increasing number of young people today are doing just that.

This is a trend that dates from the economic recession of the early 1980s, when young singles who were unable to find jobs or affordable apartments headed home until their financial conditions improved. Divorced children also came back, often bringing *their* children. Then there were—and still are—the newly married couples who either accepted Mom and Dad's invitation to live with them for a while or made the approach themselves.

"It can work," says Dr. Ruth Neubauer, former president of the New York Association for Marriage and Family Therapy, "if there are no children involved, if the husband and wife can live an independent life, and if the parents don't intrude in the marriage." As for the older generation, "I think some parents in their fifties may enjoy it, but if they're in their sixties or seventies they may feel it's a burden.

"If the younger person has made the step toward living his or her own life and is not dependent emotionally on the parents, there should be no problem. The level of independence is the key."

At best, this situation is a delicate one, and both generations have to work at it if the living arrangement is to be successful.

Certain stresses are inevitable, no matter how much goodwill exists, as each side tries to make the best of a lifestyle that probably isn't the first choice of either. The younger couple may still act more like children than adults in the presence of the older folks. The parents may feel overburdened—and take no pains to hide it. They may treat the child *like* a child. They may wonder how long they must guarantee a son or daughter—and that marriage partner, too—a home and board. When will they at last be free? What about *their* privacy and interests? They may also be concerned about their own aging parents. Caught in the middle, they may grumpily muse about when it's going to be *their* turn to be looked after.

On the other hand, a divorced or widowed parent might be delighted to have a child and his or her spouse move in for a time, just for the company. A couple coping with the burden of their own elderly or infirm parents might actually welcome sharing their problems—and some of the chores—with the younger folks.

If you think this housing style might work for you, consider your parents' or in-laws' general attitude toward you and your spouse before broaching the subject with them. Is the atmosphere between you open, relaxed, and friendly? You'll also want to be sure when you pose the question that they won't feel compelled to say yes, even if in their hearts they mean no. If you know that you'll get an honest answer from them, if you're sure you'll know how to read a tepid "okay" or be able to accept a negative decision without rancor, then it's time to consider the possibility seriously.

Where will you live in the house? Is there an existing apartment you can occupy? Can one be created, local zoning laws permitting? Will you have an entire floor to yourselves? Just a bedroom? If the folks are finding the homestead too large for them, they might want to consider converting it to a two-family house. When you move out, subsequent tenants' rents can appreciably lower their own housing costs as they near retirement.

Lori and Bill were offered two unused bedrooms in Bill's parents' home. By carving a doorway between the two rooms, the couple was able to create an attractive living room–bedroom suite. Their own entertaining was done in the living area. Bill's mom felt the arrangement was perfect for her since her two other children visited frequently, and once Lori and Bill moved, their families could occupy the rooms.

Space and privacy are the two major problems for returnees. Lori and Bill managed well with both, thanks in part to the family's disposition and the division of the upstairs into more or less separate living quarters for the newlyweds. Others might not be so fortunate.

"Each generation has to respect the privacy of the other—in sex, mail, phone conversations, and even just each couple wanting to have a talk by themselves occasionally," says Phyllis Jackson Stegall, who, with Jean Davies Okimoto, wrote *Boomerang Kids: How to Live with Adult Children Who Return Home.* "Many things that make noise can be irritating, too, such as stereos, kitchen equipment, and even coming in to the house at certain hours.

"The house and the lifestyle belong to the parents. Even if the newlywed is coming back to his or her childhood room, it's still the parents' home."

The author, a Washington State psychologist in private practice, knows whereof she speaks. Her son and daughter-in-law recently returned to her home to spend a summer. Did it work? Was it so dreadful she was driven to write a book? "It was fine," she recalls. "We have a furnished basement they used, but they had to share our kitchen. It all worked out with a good deal of patience on our part and theirs."

Lori worried about the problem of two women in the kitchen. How would she and Beverly, her mother-in-law, get along in what is still, let's face it, pretty much a one-woman domain? Beverly did not work outside the home and told Lori she would be quite happy to have dinner on the table each evening for her own husband, Sandy, and the younger couple—provided all four ate at the same hour, a reasonable stipulation. If Lori or Bill missed dinner, they could help themselves to whatever was under the tinfoil in the refrigerator. Lori and Bill offered to pay for their share of groceries, but the older couple refused, saying that rent was quite enough and, after all, the purpose of this move was to *save* money.

Still, the seeming inequity bothered Lori, especially being served dinner practically every evening (the couple tried not to eat out too often, to save money). Even doing the dishes didn't seem to be a solution, thanks to a dishwasher. So Lori usually spent part of Saturday morning preparing and freezing a stew or a vat of chili for one meal during the coming week, and perhaps making muffins (what she calls "my extremely popular every-thing-in-'em muffins") or other baked goods that could be eaten over the weekend. That contribution, she felt, was fair, since she and Bill ate breakfast at their offices and, of course, had lunch out, too.

In pondering a move home, do some number crunching, too. What is the likely price of the condo or house you hope to buy? How much will you need for a down payment? What about mortgage payments? Will you be able to afford that amount, plus other housing costs, such as real estate taxes and homeowner's insurance? How much saving will that entail and how does that translate into months (years?) spent living at "home."

Investigate at this time, too, kinds of homebuying you may not have previously considered (see Chapter 10). You may have alternatives to moving in with the folks.

Finally, consider how your marriage is likely to be affected by a year or two of living with your own or your husband's parents—especially in the early years. Will being on your own and saving over a few more years provide a happier start to your life together?

Good-nature is more agreeable in conversation than wit, and gives a certain air to the countenance which is more amiable than beauty.

Joseph Addison [1672–1719]

"I have to say I don't know where our marriage would be if we hadn't had that living area–bedroom arrangement," Lori points out. "We could get away by ourselves, watch television alone, bring our friends in without feeling we all had to socialize with Beverly and Sandy too. We really had to share nothing with them but the kitchen and the bathroom. I don't think any of this occurred to Bill, maybe because it was his home, but there I was, newly married, and sort of forced to see more of my in-laws than I would have preferred. Our arrangement was a perfect refuge for me. You can't hide out in a bedroom all the time, but with the living room attached, there was a perfect reason for me to stick to our 'quarters.' "

Be realistic about all of this. Even if the four of you are nearly perfect—hah!, right?—you're bound to get on one another's nerves from time to time. Don't let grievances mount. Dr. Neubauer cautions, "Keep a sense of humor, and remember, nobody is 100 percent secure. If you're moving back to your own home, don't feel you have to start proving yourself all over again if early issues come up and bother you."

Some points to consider as you weigh this move:

- Be upbeat once the decision is made. Don't automatically assume it's going to be a disaster.

- Heading back to *your* home? Heed Dr. Neubauer's advice, and again, don't assume the worst. Just because you and your folks didn't get along all that well when you were fifteen doesn't mean another go-round of misunderstandings and quarrels. They're older now and so are you. People mellow and change (haven't you, since then?). Give it a chance.

- Same cheery message if you're heading for your husband's former home. Forget stereotypical in-law problems. Be open-minded. In truth, your living with them may well set the stage for a more positive relationship in the future.

- Settle the logistics in advance: Who will shop and pay for groceries? Who handles the electricity bill? Heating and air-conditioning charges? What about parking the cars in the driveway? Who uses the washing machine, at which times?

- Define your turf in the house. Phyllis Jackson Stegall explains, "Whatever each family sees as its territory should be respected." Even the small stuff, like who gets first dibs on flopping on the living-room sofa at the end of the day, can be a source of contention.

- Always pay *something* for room and board. Perhaps the folks don't need your money, and may be saving it to present to you when you move. But maybe they can use your rent and will very much welcome that check. In any event, for the sake of your pride, hand something over each month.

- Don't lug back into your folks' house every item you and your husband have purchased since you first left home. Just seeing all those books, odd bits of furniture, stereo, skis, and bird-cage is likely to prove disheartening to even the most enthusiastic parents. And do they know you now have four cats? *Never* bring pets in without an invitation.

- In one way you're a guest in your parents' house, but when it comes to helping with the chores, you're certainly not. Pitch in. Bill's moving back home helped a great deal, since that big old house needed constant maintenance. "I helped Beverly with the cleaning," Lori recalls. "And I cut the grass. I know she and Sandy appreciated our help—frankly I think that's the part that made this whole thing worthwhile for them."

- Budget so the folks know you are serious about homebuying (translation: moving out). Of course everyone splurges now and then, but if they see you coming in with expensive new computer equipment, taking too many posh vacations, and generally living like the Rockefellers, they may well wonder about your future plans.

- Don't offer to redecorate for Mom or Mom-in-Law, or purchase new items for the house, unless your advice is solicited. You are a guest, after all, and your choice of, let's say, new bathroom towels may not be welcome, even though the thought may be appreciated. If, however, the older folks mention something they'd like to have for the house, buying that item for a birthday or other occasion, or perhaps no occasion at all, would be a thoughtful thing to do.

- Learn from this experience. There's a wealth of information in every house for those who are about to buy their own home.
  Carrie and Joe were each living in an apartment when they became engaged. Carrie was determined to start married life in her own house, so both moved back to their respective homes to save before the wedding. But they sort of flitted in and out of those houses, treating them almost like college dormitories. That puzzled and even annoyed Eleanor, Joe's mother. "I don't mind his coming home," she says. "But he has absolutely no idea how to run a house. We'd be happy to sit down with him and Carrie and talk about property taxes and hot-water heaters and trash collection fees, but they just show no interest. What's going to happen when they do buy

a home of their own? I suppose they'll manage through trial and error, but what a waste of an opportunity here."

• Don't fear that something is wrong with your emotional development if you are happy living with the folks. After all, this is a common lifestyle in most parts of the world—several generations under one roof. As long as you feel like an adult and are treated like one by the older generation, enjoy. Perhaps this temporary measure will evolve into a permanent, quite happy arrangement for all of you.

• Set a date for moving out, even if you have to extend that deadline. Lori and Bill moved after staying with Bill's folks for sixteen months instead of the two years they had expected. Bill's dad suffered a heart attack while they were there and retired earlier than he had planned. The two overheard the older couple talk of eventually selling the house and moving to a retirement community in a warmer climate. They felt they were standing in his parents' way at that point and decided to strike out on their own. They bought a condominium less costly than the one they had hoped to be able to purchase, but by considering the older folks and their needs, they proved to be thoughtful, caring "children." Grown-up enough to know when to move on.

"We visit them every winter," Lori says, "and we all get along famously, even in their sort of small condo. Probably because we had the experience of living together for a while and know one another's ways now. They're nice people, and I'll always be grateful to them for giving us such a good start. And frankly, since Sandy became sick, I'll always be grateful, too, that I held my tongue a few times and never caused hard feelings."

It worked for these two and it can work for you. Dr. Neubauer concludes: "Both sides must want it because they have become friends and people who can talk to one another."

8

WHEN IT'S TIME TO BUY

How will you know when the time is right for you to buy a house or condominium? When your savings balance says you can? When your personal life gives you the green light? When the national economy and real estate market in your area are telling you to buy, buy, buy? Or perhaps a little of all three?

Aside from the people mentioned in Chapter 1 who prefer renting their home or would be wiser to do so, most Americans who are tenants want to own the roof over their heads as soon as they can manage that purchase. A home of one's own has always been a dream in this country, and it's one realized by more than 60 percent of Americans.

With your own place, you are no longer at the mercy of a landlord's whims. There is no need to walk across floors softly if you choose not to, to keep the music down, to restrict the number of pets you own. You do not have to worry about rent increases, or whether your building will be "going condo" when you do not want to buy your apartment. A home of your own will bring you space and privacy, certainly more of each than you would find living as a tenant. There may be a backyard, too. If you are creative, you can put your talents to work decorating any way you choose, without worrying about restrictions in the lease.

You will have that sense of permanence and stability that homeownership brings. It is in some ways an indefinable pride— "putting my feet under my own table" is the way many men of a few generations back expressed it.

Though one can certainly "settle down," while living in an apartment, buying a home means an even greater commitment to a community. You cannot help becoming at least minimally involved, thanks to the homework you will have done in preparing to buy—not much of which would have particularly interested you if you were hunting for a rental apartment. Consider: What is the economic makeup of this town? Is there industry that helps support it or is income from new, tax-paying businesses badly needed? What are the real estate taxes? How are the schools? Under what form of government does the town operate? Is there a master plan for growth? Is there a newspaper? Finding answers to these questions familiarizes you with your new town and helps you see yourself in the near future as a contributing resident. You learn of social, cultural, and religious issues or programs that may draw you into volunteer work. You see shops that interest you. Maybe there is a university offering evening courses or other educational opportunities.

Once you buy your home, your stake in the community becomes important. You want that town to be the best it can be. In part, its success reflects well on you, but you also have a natural concern about the major investment you have made by purchasing a home there.

Owning a home presents most Americans not only with their largest investment but also with their best opportunity for tax benefits. Mortgage interest is deductible from federal tax returns, and in the first several years of a mortgage, you are paying virtually all interest and very little principal. Real estate taxes are also deductible, in full. Both deductions are what drives many renters into homeownership. They need those attractive tax breaks!

This is a leveraged investment, too, which means spending the least amount of your money to purchase the most you can. Let's say you buy a home for $100,000, with a down payment of $15,000. Its value appreciates only 3 percent the first year, so it is now worth $103,000. The next year it appreciates 4 percent. Now the market value is $107,120. In two years, your $15,000 investment has brought you $7,120 in profit. And those are conservative figures. Some homes bring their owners far more in appreciation for the few years they hold on to them.

A home is also a forced savings, another bonus for most Americans. A home loan is generally amortized. That means it is paid in full over its allotted term in equal payments that include both principal and interest. Each time you make a monthly payment, you are paying the interest for the preceding month. The balance of the payment is applied to the loan's principal amount. So every month the amount applied to principal increases and the amount applied to interest decreases. That's why in the early years of your loan, you are paying off very little principal, while in the later years most of your payment goes toward principal.

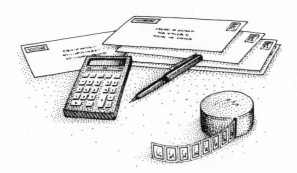

During the paying off of a mortgage you are building important equity—the difference between the market value of the home and what is owed against it, such as a mortgage. Decreasing the mortgage increases your equity, and so does market appreciation of your house. While you were a renter, you had nothing to show, in terms of an investment, at the end of a year. With a home you have that savings, intangible as it may seem and illiquid as it certainly is (you cannot convert your home to cash quickly, as you can with many other investments).

A home is also a hedge against inflation. Just think how prices of housing have risen since your parents bought their first home. Unlike other valuable possessions, such as automobiles, some jewelry, and furs, homes almost always sell for more than one pays for them. It may seem that the price of the house where you live now cannot possibly rise any higher. But it probably will. The home you buy today will be worth more, if not next year, then certainly a few years down the road. It will be the best saving, the best investment, you are likely ever to make.

A word of warning, however: you are buying, it is hoped, to have an attractive place in which to live, not to make a quick killing with your investment. Except for towns that might be considered "hot spots" around the country, residential real estate is not appreciating at the dramatically high levels of the late 1970s anymore. It is understandable that you might want to buy virtually anything you can afford just to enter the ranks of homeowner. You may think that, after you have bought, you can hold on to that house for a year or two or three, watch it *rapidly* appreciate and then trade up to the kind of home you both really want. This may not happen! It costs money to buy a home, as you will see, and money to move, and equity builds slowly in a market where homes appreciate only at the low rate of inflation that exists these days. If you want to sell in a year or two, you may not be able to get back your investment, let alone make a profit. So buying a home *only* as an investment gamble is unrealistic, and can be a dangerous ploy.

From the broader national picture to your own personal situation: Is this the time for the two of you to buy?

- If your careers are relatively stable, with no relocation looming;

- if you truly want to buy a house, find yourselves shopping around on weekends, visiting open houses and reading the real estate advertisements in local papers, "just for fun";

- if you badly need the tax break homeownership brings to two-career couples;

- if mortgage rates are not sky-high, and houses in your area are reasonably affordable (you should be looking at homes priced from two to no more than three times your gross income; if that means a top price for you of $135,000, and you are in an outrageously expensive housing market where that amount is not likely to bring you a house, you may have to confine yourselves to the condo supply, if *that* is possible)—

—then it sounds as if you are ready to take on the mantle of homeowner. There is just one other point.

Can You Afford a Home?

All the desire in the world cannot bring you a home if the numbers do not work. There are four major financial points to take into account (aside from the housing prices, of course). The last one may not have occurred to you, but it has sunk many first-time buyers into a sea of debt and bills, erasing any pleasure in homeowning.

1. *The Down Payment*   Most lenders require at least 10 percent nowadays, with more common demands at 15 to 20 percent down. So if you are looking at a $100,000 home, you may be required to come up with $10,000 to *$20,000,* a staggering amount. There is more about the down payment, and how to put one together, in Chapter 13.

2. *The Mortgage*   The cost of owning a home is 30 to 35 percent of a borrower's income. Can you afford that much for housing, or are you burdened with too many other sizable expenses? Perhaps there are college loans, or child-support payments, or perhaps both of your incomes are still in the starter-salary range. Lenders grant mortgages for, broadly speaking, homes costing two to two and a half times a household income. If your joint income is, let's say, $35,000, the top end of that range would allow you to purchase a home for about $85,000. Perhaps you are unfortunate enough to live in a region of the country where housing is far more expensive than that. That sum may buy you only an extremely small, unattractive condominium or cooperative in an elderly building in the process of being converted from rental units. You may not want to buy there.

   What has happened is that you have been, like a growing number of your fellow, young first-time buyers, priced out of the market. There *are* ways around this, however, including programs aimed at first-timers. These are coming up in succeeding chapters, so do not write off buying at this juncture just because the numbers are depressing.

3. *The Closing Costs*   These are fees involved in the transfer of property from the seller to the buyer. They range from 3 to 5 percent of the loan (more about them in Chapter 16), they must be paid up front, and there is no way to get around them. If you are securing a $90,000 mortgage, then you might expect to pay between $2,700 and $4,500 in settlement charges.

That makes the down payment and the closing costs sums of money you must have on hand up front, at the time of purchase. (While calculating, note that you will have to have available $100 to $300 for a mortgage application fee, and 1 to 2 percent of the purchase price as an "earnest money" deposit on the house you decide to buy. More detailed explanations of both charges are found in upcoming chapters.)

4. *The Hidden Expenses*   These are what no one tells you about, not even your mother. To be truthful, they probably do not occur to anyone. They are the trivia of homeowning, certainly not in the same class as that mammoth concern—securing, and being able to pay, the mortgage. Still, you will see how these bills can eat away at your budget.

The hidden expenses include making regular (usually quarterly) payments of real estate taxes on your home. Property taxes may be low where you are looking, perhaps only several hundred dollars a year. More likely, they will cost over $1,000, and maybe more than $5,000. You will also have to meet an annual homeowner's insurance premium (more about that in Chapter 14) and the premium for private mortgage insurance if you carry that as well (see Chapter 15). *Each* of those fees can run from $300 to just under $1,000 annually. You will have to pay a water bill to your municipal authority, too, perhaps quarterly. That charge varies widely. It could be as little as $50 annually or could amount to several hundred dollars. Also, there is heat. Perhaps you did not pay for the gas, oil, or electric heat in your apartment. Now you will be faced with a sizable bill for heating your home. How sizable? From $1,000 to $3,000, or more, each year.

You may have a monthly condominium maintenance fee where you live, and other charges such as trash collection and sewerage fees.

The folks at the local hardware store will certainly become acquainted with the new couple in town. You will be making many trips there for start-up purchases for your new home—everything from trash cans, a rake, lawnmower, and snow shovel to window shades, keys, smoke detectors, and the myriad other items you will see that you absolutely must have. Perhaps you do not already own a refrigerator and will have to buy one, and maybe a clothes washer, too, if the laundromat is several miles away. There is no dollar figure you can apply in advance to this miscellany, but you can see how quickly these store bills—and credit card balances—mount.

Good grief, you are probably saying about now. This is more than we expected. Yes, homeowning costs are frequently a revelation to first-time buyers. But in the main, if you can afford it, ownership does pay off, in dollars and cents and intangibly, in achieving one of your principal goals as a couple. What it takes is knowledge of the market, so that you go into this exciting new venture with the greatest likelihood of success. This is likely to happen if you carefully read, and apply to your own lives, the material on househunting and financing your purchase that is coming up in the next several chapters.

Are you sold? Or . . .

WHAT ARE YOUR REASONS FOR BUYING?

	VERY IMPORTANT	FAIRLY IMPORTANT	DOESN'T MATTER
Investment (appreciation, equity growth)			
Status			
Tax benefits			
Space			
Privacy			
Yard, grounds			
Sense of community			
Meeting and becoming friendly with neighbors			
Planning a home-based business			
Wanting to start a family			
Lower costs than renting			
Stability of regular housing payments (mortgage)			
Creativity in decorating			
Security			
Better lifestyle (more entertaining, room for overnight guests, etc.)			

9

ARE YOU NERVOUS ABOUT ALL THIS?

It's all right if you are. A certain degree of "My God, what are we getting into!" is normal. After all, a home is the major purchase of one's life, and somehow, just as the second trip to Europe seems to come more easily than the first, and the second job is less difficult to find than the first, so buying the second and third and succeeding houses is not quite the trauma that buying the first one is.

So, you're tense. Are you as fearful as Jenny and Phil, who lived in an apartment for the first three years of their marriage and, despite two sets of parents willing to help financially, and despite a joint income of more than $60,000, kept putting off that major purchase?

"We went through developments and we went to open houses," Jenny says. "But there was just this block, and Phil had it, too. It seemed like these houses were for other people, not us. No matter how affordable or how luxurious they were, we couldn't identify with owning them ourselves."

Some fears about this major step are normal. Indeed, if you did not feel some trepidation, you probably would not be taking this buying business seriously enough. But when a normal fear gets in the way and you can't progress to what you think the next stage of your life should be, or when you are truly trapped in a housing situation you find unpleasant or downright intolerable and you just can't *do* anything to get out of it, then you have a problem.

It's not insoluble. Let's take your fears and analyze them. By taking them apart, they may fall apart, and you will see that you will get through this rite of passage just as you have others in your lifetime. And the rewards that wait on the other end—well, an analogy might be cold feet before the wedding, another quite legitimate state. But you went through with it, jitters and all, and now—look at the rewards!

The fears of homebuying can be broken down as follows:

1. *"What's going on in the world makes me nervous—there are too many things that are beyond my control."*

Yes, the stock market did crash, and more recently than the big crash in 1929. This is a legitimate cause for concern. But the crash of 1987 had no serious long-term effect on the national economy. If your fears fall into this category, remember that homes are not subject to the high market sensitivity that short-term investments like stocks are. Homes are bought principally as places for people to live, although all buyers hope they are making good investments as well. The real estate market can react to a poor economy, but the lines on the seismograph do not fluctuate wildly. In a recession, people will hold on to their homes until conditions improve. There is no panic-selling.

To further reassure you: after the Great Depression, economic safeguards, such as Social Security and unemployment insurance, were put into place, so that a mass wipeout of individual assets is not as likely to occur. Houses lost in those days had mortgage terms that were usually set at five years, not the long-term loans we have today.

Worried you may not be able to sell your home for what you paid, plus a little profit? A legitimate concern. But then, most of us will hold on to our houses until the economy improves and we can get the price we seek. Only in a rare emergency situation might you have to sell quickly, and if the emergency is a job transfer, your company may well pay for any losses you sustain.

Basically, if you have chosen the house—and particularly the location—well, you should have no trouble come resale time, even if you have to wait out a season or two of slight economic slump. It will rebound.

By all means do keep an eye on the economy, though, even as you househunt. Good bargains can often be found in an economic downturn, when some sellers *must* sell their homes. But when the news from Wall Street is gloomy, don't think that you and your house are going to be tumbling down the financial tubes. It just won't happen.

A small P.S. here. Of course, you and your husband may work in the financial arena, or a field similarly sensitive to volatile fluctuations. If your jobs could be lost in an economic recession or short-term crash, or if you sense that they could be on the block during any downturn, that's another story. Then you may well prefer to watch the market far more intently than your fellow househunters or homeowners employed in other professions.

2. *"Real estate in general makes me twitch. It's a totally new area for me, and I know nothing about it."*

Maybe you don't—but you can learn. If you talk to real estate agents, read on the subject (as you're doing now), drive around and familiarize yourself with houses and with neighborhoods, talk to friends and business associates who have bought, it will all come together. Soon you will realize you know more each weekend you head out househunting. (Good news: you really only have to learn about this once. The second and third homes will be bought based on the same information, perhaps changed only a little to reflect market conditions at the time.)

A mortgage is *scary,* whether it's for $50,000 or $150,000. If it's more than you have in savings—and for most of us it certainly is—then you have a right to be nervous about being in debt for so much money. But mortgages are carried by more than half of America's households, and homes can't be paid for in five years (by most buyers, anyway). So a mortgage is an acceptable debt, and, fortunately, can be paid off at a reasonably affordable rate each month.

If it's *seeking* a mortgage that scares you, remember that here, too, the news is good. More than 85 percent of mortgage applications are approved. Lenders are in the business of lending money—or where would they be? In most economies, they welcome your interest. Perhaps you will not qualify for as much money as you would like, but if you have a reasonable income and good credit, you can buy *something.* It will almost certainly not be the home of your dreams. First-time houses or condominiums usually are not.

Confused about what to buy? That can be settled by exploring neighborhoods and housing styles. Maybe you will find the suburban single-family house not at all "you." You're country folk. Or you are strictly cliff dwellers and will not look beyond city limits. In town, you may decide on a condominium or perhaps a single-family row house. Or maybe you will opt for the two-family house and become a landlord. All of this will come into focus as you see home styles you do *not* want. Little by little, one style will emerge that feels right for you.

Jenny concedes that that was pretty much the problem she and Phil were having. They were unable to picture themselves living in a rambling suburban house, yet thought that when one buys, one automatically heads for a ranch or a split-level on a quarter-acre lot. That's what "buying a house" means, they'd reasoned. Then she began to realize that that picture is not for everyone. She and Phil went on house tours in their city, were attracted to lofts, and have recently purchased one.

NO NEED TO WORRY	LEGITIMATE CONCERN
• The national economy will completely collapse, taking your investment with it.	• You are buying more house than you can comfortably afford.
• You will never find a home that you like in your price range.	• You both hold volatile jobs that could be lost in a severe economic downturn. (Yet even this doesn't have to mean foregoing homeownership; just proceed with caution.)
• You will find it impossible to maintain a home—make repairs, keep mechanical systems working, etc.	• You do not like the home you have chosen, but are buying it because it's all you can afford, *he* likes it, etc.
• You will be unable to secure a mortgage (the overwhelming number of applicants do).	• You will make several wrong moves in the buying process; you will be "taken" somewhere along the way because you have not prepared for this step. (Solution: doing homework to familiarize yourself with houses, mortgages, and so on.)
• Maybe the time just isn't right for this step. (If you want to buy, can afford a home, and the economy favors buyers, then go ahead; you just have cold feet.)	• You will be moving too quickly after buying to recoup your investment from this purchase, let alone make any profit on it.

Not at all traditional, but perhaps that's why they were fighting househunting. They did not *want* to buy what they thought they *had* to buy.

"What if we sign papers saying we will buy a house, and then change our minds?" you may also wonder.

You can get around that by signing a "binder," not a more formal contract of sale. This process is explained in Chapter 12.

If you get cold feet on Monday, after walking through a house you wanted and signed a binder for on Sunday, visit the house again. Work the numbers again, too, if it's the mortgage payment that bothers you.

Even if you sign a *contract,* you can have two contingencies written in (or more, if the seller agrees). Usually the sale going through is dependent on your being able to secure financing, so that worry is eliminated. You can also specify you want a home inspection, the results of which must be satisfactory to you. If you are worried about the inner workings of the house, a contingency clause should alleviate *that* concern.

3. *"There are things in my own life and background that cause me to worry about buying and owning a home."*

What concerns you? The fact that you've lived in apartments all your working life? The fact that while you lived at home you paid no attention to the workings of a house—and now you wonder if you will be able to maintain the home you buy? You'll worry about every clang and creak and squeak?

A legitimate nail-biter. But "homeowner" is a role you will grow into. The day you take ownership of the place you buy, you will be handed the keys and will at least know how to open the door(s)! From there you will acquire more and more knowledge. How? By living through experiences and figuring things out and asking neighbors and asking at the hardware store and asking your folks or his how *they* handled one problem or another. You will grow into being a capable homeowner the way you grew into other situations in your life, such as your career and *its* responsibilities. Look at it from the perspective of the househunter and it seems overwhelming. Take it a step—and a creak and a drip—at a time, and it's manageable.

Maintenance very definitely worried Kerrie, who married at twenty after spending eighteen years at her parents' home and a year and a half in a college dormitory. But Doug was thirty-one, and had bounced around from one apartment to another for almost a decade. He wanted a home and was able to afford one.

"We went with a condominium," Kerrie recalls of that purchase three years ago. "Doug knew I didn't know beans about houses, and while we were talking about buying he told me he would be a little concerned about me alone in a big house at night. He's a teacher, and has some evening classes and also does a little consulting work at night. I worried about that, too, but didn't want to say anything. So the compromise we reached was the condo. There's little maintenance for me, and I've learned enough about what I have to do so that when we do move from here I'll be more confident. Doug's happy because there are people around me and I'm not isolated on some suburban street. Frankly, that makes me happy, too. We don't even talk about moving, although I suppose we will someday."

If maintenance worries you both, or if you feel that the upkeep of a house will be almost impossible with the lives you lead at work (and the desire you both have for a little fun on weekends), by all means look at the condominium or cooperative. Avoid the fixer-upper, and skip the two-family house. You probably won't even consider building one yourselves. The single-family house may be fine for you if it's in mint condition, and learning can be done at your leisure. Kerrie's situation involved a concern for being alone many evenings, but she could have managed a house that was in good shape. But—and why are there so many sides to this question?—just as you don't have to know what makes a car tick to know how to drive, you don't have to know what makes a heating system run, or what's going on in hidden pipelines, to keep a house maintained, either. You don't absolutely have to *throw* yourselves into the role of homeowner. Just pick up enough to get by. Knowing how to recognize when something's not quite right—and who to call to fix it—will do fine.

But what if you don't like the house after you've bought it? This is Jan's fear, one she has not shared with her husband of two years, Tony. She masks her concern about buying with the fact that just now Tony is working at two jobs and, she tells him, he will be too tired to bother with a house. In reality, she concedes, "I worry that we'll buy and then I'll see a house I like better and I'll be totally turned off by the one we have. Or there will be one thing wrong with it that I won't notice until after we're in and *then* I'll be turned off by it. I know myself and I know how changeable I am. About the only thing I've stayed stable on is liking Tony. Clothes, careers, where to go on a vacation, I'm always changing my mind."

This one is a toughie, because one does not quickly change houses, without risking the loss of tens of thousands of dollars in the transaction. Jan would be wise to have a little talk with herself, and realize that a home is a far more important purchase than clothes or vacations; once the decision is made to buy *that* house, she and Tony are committed. What may make homebuying a little different for Jan is the legality of the process, the amount of money involved, and the slowness of the selling process. Jan can surely tell herself she can stay in a home with a flaw or two for a couple of years (or why not concentrate on fixing the flaw, if it can be done?). If Tony is equally disenchanted, of course, they can both talk about moving. Since the average American moves six to ten times in a lifetime, another move for the two of them would not be out of the norm. Just so long as it's one they both want, and they agree to hold out if the economy slumps temporarily, so they stand to make the most profit from the transaction.

Another personal fear of some homebuyers is that once they've signed all the papers and moved into the home, they will find they can't afford it! That is not a fear to spend much time worrying about. Mortgage lenders do not issue loans for more than they think customers can carry. *However,* and this is a big However. The mortgage lender will not know that once you're in the home, you'll be heading for the posh furniture store at the mall to run up several thousand dollars' worth of furnishings. And that maybe you'll buy a second car, too, since you're in the country now. All of that may well push your finances to the wall and you will be strapped. But the house itself should not be beyond your means. You will just have to take it easy when trying to turn it into an *Architectural Digest* layout. First-time buyers find they must budget very carefully since there is *so* much they need, so many plans they have for the place, so many rooms to fill—and so little discretionary income.

That's it. Maybe now you will find yourself a little less nervous about this Big Step, even though some legitimate concerns remain. That's natural. Just don't let unnecessary fears stand in the way of your buying the nicest, most affordable home you can.

10

CONDO?
RESALE HOME?
TWO-FAMILY
HOUSE?
A GUIDE
TO WHAT YOU
CAN BUY

So what is your first home going to be? Are you thinking automatically about a condominium, or perhaps a resale single-family house? Either would make an excellent starter home, but why not explore other options as well? One of the housing styles that follow could also be a smart investment, as well as an attractive, even delightful, place in which to live during the early years of your marriage.

THE CONDOMINIUM

Nowadays considered *the* starter home, with condo units virtually everywhere in the country and in price ranges for every income.

In a condominium you purchase your apartment outright, secure your own mortgage, and pay your own real estate taxes on that unit. As a member of the owners' association, you also own an undivided interest in the common areas of the building or complex—hallways, grounds, parking garage, and the like. These are maintained by the monthly fee all residents pay to the owners' association, which every buyer must join. So you will be making a monthly mortgage payment, plus paying real estate taxes and homeowner's insurance, *plus* a monthly maintenance fee to the association. Depending on the luxury level of the complex you have chosen, that fee can run from as little as $50 or so to several hundred dollars.

Condominiums, when properly chosen, can be wise investments and can provide a pleasant lifestyle, especially for a working couple who have no interest in maintenance chores. Some of the more luxurious communities sport pools, tennis courts, and lively social programs, another boon to those who prefer relaxing to raking leaves. Buying a condominium can ease you both into homeowning, since you will still basically live in an apartment, only this one you'll own. A few points to bear in mind, however:

- A condominium is a form of housing ownership; "townhomes" are an architectural style—usually two- or three-story condominiums attached to one another like row housing. When you see townhomes advertised, they are almost always condos. A "town house" is usually an urban row house, although in some parts of the country developers may use "town house" when referring to these condominium communities.

- One difficulty that *might* crop up for the two of you, especially if you are used to a few years of apartment living, is adopting a different mind set about your home. Yes, it is an apartment and your building or complex looks like other apartments you have lived in or visited, but this time you *own*. Some renters have a hard time with this and expect someone else to attend to such matters as taking care of the trash cans, reporting vandalism, and the like. But this is your home, and while no one is suggesting that you run for president of the owners' association, you *will* have to contribute more than benign neglect to your community. There is no longer a landlord to whom you can turn. Members of owners' associations tell many stories of new residents who complain to the association when an electrical outlet doesn't work in their apartment or their room air-conditioner is broken. One couple even complained to their association that their telephone was broken!

- Condo living requires that you conform somewhat to the prevailing style. You almost certainly will not be allowed to alter the exterior of your unit, so if you are highly imaginative and want your shutters painted a color different from the others, or want to put pink flamingos on your front lawn, you may well be forbidden to do so by the owners' association. Inside your apartment, of course, it's a different story—bring on the flamingos! (A remodeling job as major as knocking down walls, however, may require permission from the owner's association.)

- Look to the resale value of your apartment. If the area is overbuilt, you may not be able to sell as quickly as you would like, at the price you are seeking, when you want to move on.

- The brand-new complexes are not necessarily the best. Some communities that have been around for fifteen or twenty years and have good reputations may turn out to be a wiser investment, come resale time.

THE RESALE HOUSE

This is where most househunters head—newlyweds and everyone else. These are existing houses found everywhere in all price ranges and of every vintage, from two-hundred-year-old farmhouses to two-year-old split-levels. You are almost certain to find a resale house you can afford. Generally speaking, these homes can be purchased for at least $20,000 less than a brand-new site-built home. Older houses can be long on charm, with architectural details and construction materials of the highest quality, the sort of craftsmanship that can no longer be duplicated. But old houses have their problems, too. Marble mantels do not age, but heating and electrical systems do. So while you may find a resale home at a good price, you may also need to spend quite a few dollars to fix it up—and still more money to keep it maintained.

Some additional thoughts:

- If you find an affordable house, will you need a home-improvement loan to make it livable? Can you make loan payments, plus meet the monthly mortgage, pay real estate taxes and other housing-related expenses? (Investigate the special 203K program offered by the U.S. Department of Housing and Urban Development [HUD], which offers a mortgage *and* home-improvement loan as one package. There are no restrictions for applicants.)

- Be careful about the neighborhood. Some, especially in urban areas, are on the decline. Some have bottomed out and are on the way back, while still others have always been stable, changing little over the decades. Knowing which is which can make your investment a great one or a disaster. Look for an enclave that has a block or neighborhood association—always a sign that owners *care*. In areas you're not sure about, keep an eye out for indicators that a renaissance is under way, like flower boxes, gas lamps, or trendy shops opening nearby. Read local papers, not just the real estate advertisements, but the real estate *articles* that talk about neighborhoods that are being revived.

- Always, *always* have an older house inspected before buying it, a point that will be made again, and explained in more detail in Chapter 12.

THE BRAND-NEW SINGLE-FAMILY HOME

This is the first choice of a great many househunters, although these days most of them cannot afford the price of site-built construction. Or can they?

Check new developments in your area. Perhaps you can afford one of the brand-new townhome communities, but single-family houses are likely to carry much higher price tags, because of their extra space and the high cost of land, which is an expense the builder passes along to buyers.

Site-built homes, where the developer actually constructs that ten-room colonial right on the lot, cost more than manufactured houses, which arrive at the building site in sections and then are assembled. Manufactured homes, depending on the company making them and the building turning them into houses, can be an excellent investment. Often it is hard to tell them from homes down the street that were built brick by brick.

Think about this:

- You may want to ask the developer of the community where you are looking if there are some bonuses for buying there— for instance: lower financing through his own mortgage lender; a lower down payment; carpeting, higher-quality appliances, or some other attractive extra thrown in at no additional cost. Builders getting new communities off the ground, or those eager to close a development that's just about sold out, are often eager to make concessions to buyers. Check newspaper advertisements, too. Sometimes builders in a slow market announce "Will Pay Closing Costs" or "$1,500 Bonus until June 30" or offer some other inducement to spur sales. The new home, depending on its location and what the developer is offering, can be expensive, but with a little bargaining on your part, and knowledge of the community where you are hunting, you may well be able to pull off quite a coup for yourselves.

- A brand-new house is not always "worth" more than a resale home. Which constitutes the better investment again depends on the magic word: "location." The most lavish newly built French château–style house on an acre lot is not going to attract many buyers with open checkbooks if it's next to a landfill area or a Burger King or fronts on U.S. 1. So in comparing the resale value of one with that of the other, you must consider location, in addition to whether the old house is in good condition, and indeed whether the new one is! More than one brand-new home suffers from cracked walls, serious drainage problems, unnatural settling, and other maladies, thanks to shoddy construction.

Also, fortunately for the real estate market and for all buyers, some folks will always prefer age in a home, and those nice details like sun porches, french doors, and little nooks under the stairway. Others will go for the brand-new—the home *so* new it is still surrounded by a sea of construction mud. Each house must be weighed on its own merits.

THE TWO-FAMILY HOUSE

This could be a four-star investment for the two of you, and might make the cost of owning your own home practically negligible. Too often the two-family house is overlooked by house-hunters, whether they are first-time buyers or not.

Frequently, for the same price you'd pay for a one-family home, you can purchase a house that comes with an income-producing unit. Let's say the rent on that unit—and it can be a small apartment in the basement or two floors in a four-story, two-apartment house—is $600 a month. The monthly mortgage payment for the house is $900. The income, and savings to you, is obvious.

What turns some buyers away from this purchase is becoming a landlord. True, there is work involved in that role—selecting tenants, keeping the apartment in good shape, and the like. But most who buy this type of investment property say it all becomes worthwhile on the first of each month when that rent check comes in!

Carla and Larry grew up and married in a stable, inner-city neighborhood and wanted to remain there, with family and friends nearby. Most of the homes there were large, however, and many of them had been converted over the years to rooming houses or homes with one, two, or even three apartments.

The couple lived in an apartment after their wedding, but only a few short months later were hit by the "buying" bug.

"I saw how popular this town was becoming, with new people moving in all the time," Carla recalls. "I said to Larry, 'We'd better buy before the prices go so high we won't be able to.' Both of us were determined to stay here."

The couple, both twenty-eight at the time, bought a small two-family house. It is fifteen feet wide, with three floors for them and a very small apartment in the basement for a tenant (the tenant has only a portion of the basement because there's a laundry room there, too, for the owner). Carla has landscaped the yard and put out lawn furniture, and although the tenant is welcome there, she has never put foot on a blade of grass. They have all been there three years now. "I'll tell you," Carla continues, "if you're nervous about buying a home, you probably won't be any more nervous about becoming a landlord, too, so go ahead and do both. It's worked out well for us, although we have family here—and friends, too—who have apartments in their houses, so we know where to go when we have questions. We have a very nice young girl living downstairs, very quiet, travels with her job pretty often. We feed her cat when she's away, and when we're away she comes up and feeds our three. In fact, when she's out, we leave her apartment door open (with her permission) and her cat travels between her place and ours. She also takes in the mail and waters the plants when we're on vacation.

"We've had no problem with repairs on the house—we fix anything that breaks in her apartment the same way we would anything that breaks in ours.

"One other thing I have my eye on—Larry's mother and my mother are both widows. We don't have any plans to move from here, and if either of them gets to the point where she can't live alone, she can move into that apartment one day. She can have her own place and her independence, and yet be there for Larry and me to keep an eye on."

Some points to consider:

- If you are a marginal mortgage applicant, falling short in one area or another—perhaps you have not been working very long, have a poor credit history or none at all—a mortgage lender is likely to take into account the rent coming in from that rental unit, which may well push your application for a loan into the "approved" column.

- Besides a rent check, ownership of a two-family house brings other financial benefits. There are tax considerations for those owning income-producing property. Your repairs to the tenant's unit are deductible, for instance, and even if you put a new roof on your house, the percentage of the house that you rent out can be deducted from that roof charge.

- You will have to acquaint yourselves with local renting laws before you *bid* on a house. You don't want to buy an expensive one to find that the tenant is paying $125 a month and is protected by rent-control statutes.

- Resale? Two- and three-family houses tend to sell a little more slowly than a single-family house, but that has no effect on the profit you are likely to make if you have chosen the house and the location well. Still, if you expect a job transfer to another city, keep this in mind. The house may be on the market longer than another type you might buy.

THE COOPERATIVE

Not nearly as numerous as condominiums, co-ops are another form of homeownership that means apartment living with a group of like-minded unit owners.

Cooperatives can be buildings where units are sold at market rates (these are usually found in urban areas), or they can be limited-profit co-ops, where residents are allowed to walk away with minimal gain so the housing is kept affordable. The third style is government-assisted co-ops, which have federal rules governing admissions, fees, and nonprofit status. You are more likely to come across the first or second in your househunt—open-market co-ops in larger cities, limited-profit ones in small towns and rural areas.

Cooperatives work like this: You buy shares in the corporation that owns the building and holds the mortgage. In return for your purchase you are given a proprietary lease that allows you to live in your unit. The number of your shares may be in proportion to the size of your apartment, or perhaps everyone has the same number of shares, from the penthouse dweller to the studio resident. In some buildings, having more shares means having more votes, in others, one apartment equals one vote.

Prospective buyers must be approved by the co-op's board of directors. Which is one facet of life in this housing style that makes it different from a condominium, where anyone is free to buy, without approval from the owners' association.

The other major difference is that a cooperative is considered personal, not real, property. The condominium is real estate, and you have a deed to your property the way any other homeowner would. If you must finance your co-op unit, you do so with a personal, or special co-op, loan. There is no mortgage.

Can this be a good deal for you? Of course, if the building is a solid one—not just in construction, but in its board of directors and its financial statement. Here, too, a lot depends on location. Buying an open-market cooperative *can* pay off when you sell, the way any other home purchase would.

Lisa lives with her husband, Marv, in a limited-profit cooperative house in a small town in the West. She is a writer; Marv teaches in a local private school. Their financial profile (not a grandiose joint income—about $25,000 a year) is such that they were approved for residence in a small building that is run as a limited-profit cooperative corporation. They have a floor-through apartment in one of the houses, for which they made a $3,500 down payment, and now pay $400 a month, which includes their share of the co-op's mortgage, real estate taxes, and operating expenses. The couple pay for their own utilities.

Like other homeowners, they are allowed income-tax deductions for their share of mortgage interest and real estate tax payments.

When Lisa and Marv move, they will be given back their initial $3,500, plus interest, and the apartment reverts to the corporation, to be passed along to the next "tenants." The monthly maintenance charge they pay, not so incidentally, is substantially lower than the rent they would be charged on the open market in their community.

"This is just something for our life right now," Lisa says. "We don't have enough for a home, and we're not sure we want to stay here anyway. Marv talks about leaving teaching and I think I'm about ready for a change, too, although I don't know what kind of switch I'll make. But we enjoy this kind of life and have made real friends in the houses. That $3,500 is earning us five percent interest for every year we're here, so we'll have that, plus what we're saving, to put on a house whenever we do decide to leave."

There's more to consider:

- Life in a co-op is not too different from life in a condo, in that you pay a monthly maintenance fee to the corporation, which you will have to add to your calculations. In a co-op, that fee includes real estate taxes, however; whereas in a condo, you pay those taxes yourself on your own unit.

- Which is the better investment, the co-op or the condo? A difficult question. If chosen carefully, both can pay you back handsomely come resale time. The condo may be slightly more popular because it *is* real estate, and because the absence of the need for approval by a board of directors presumably makes it easier to sell. However, in urban areas like New York City, Chicago, Miami, and some others, there is no question about the appeal of the co-op. In New York City, in fact, there are hundreds more co-ops than condos.

IF THAT'S A "RANCH," THEN WHAT'S A "RAISED RANCH"?

How to tell home styles while reading real estate ads:

COLONIAL   Usually a large two-story house with four bedrooms, two and a half baths, and an architectural style that boasts pillars or at least a center entrance.

SPLIT-LEVEL   Often found in developments; here the living area, kitchen, and dining room are on the main level, with bedrooms a half flight up, and a family room and the garage a half flight down.

RANCH   Became popular in the 1950s and 1960s, and refers to a house built on one level.

EXPANDED RANCH   The little ranch that grew—extra bedrooms added upstairs, Cape Cod–style with dormer windows.

RAISED RANCH OR BILEVEL   A house where the entry foyer is between floors. Upstairs you have the traditional ranch, downstairs is a family room, maybe an extra bedroom, laundry room, and the garage. No basement.

CAPE COD   Small, square houses. If there are upstairs bedrooms, they have pitched roofs and dormers.

MOTHER-DAUGHTER   Refers to a house where the owner has created a full separate apartment. Usually, if it is identified this way, the flat must be rented to a member of the family.

CONTEMPORARY   Likely to mean sleek and relatively new, with cathedral ceilings, lots of glass, and of stone or wood construction. Popular in the West and Southwest, although, of course, it can be constructed anywhere.

DUTCH COLONIAL, TUDOR, NORMANDY CASTLE   Usually your basic four-bedroom, two-story "colonial" floor plan with an interesting (sometimes artificially bizarre) façade designed to attract buyers.

THE MOBILE HOME

No, they are not "trailers" anymore. In fact, over the last decade or so, they have undergone such a change that the industry's manufacturers' association is even confused about the term "mobile home," and sometimes just calls them "manufactured houses."

What has happened is that the lowly tin trailers in a sort of seedy "camp" on the main drag in many towns across America have evolved into "communities" where homes look as attractive as any single-family detached house, where streets are nicely landscaped and there are sidewalks, too. Often there are pools and clubhouses and security guards at the gate. Prices can run well into six figures. This is a mobile home?

Yes and no. Some parks—or at least their residents—call them "mobiles," but the newer houses *are* manufactured homes. There are no axles under them to make them motor vehicles, as earlier trailers were. Indeed, today's mobiles aren't going anywhere. So if residents of Rolling Clouds Park want to move, they sell and buy elsewhere. No such thing as hitching up *these* mobiles and taking them with you!

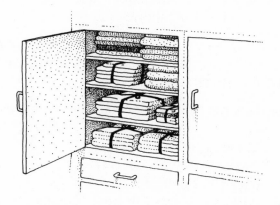

Mobile parks have traditionally been for newlyweds and senior citizens, the former starting up and waiting until they can afford more house, the latter paring down and being quite happy with the smaller space of the "trailer." In some of the older parks around the country, you will still find that same mix. But the newer communities, with the sprawling homes, are likely to attract people of all ages and lifestyles. If mobile-home parks are popular where you are, you may well want to consider one as a starter home.

Points to ponder:

- To increase the value of your purchase, try to move into an attractive community, with double-width and perhaps triple-width units. The old single-width trailer tends to depreciate the way an automobile does—which is to say, you take a loss, sometimes a substantial one, when you sell. The larger homes in the four-star parks can appreciate in value the way any home might. The key here is how attractive the mobile community is and how much in demand its homes are—or that old "location" angle again.

- It is now possible to secure a mortgage for homes in some of these communities, especially the ones that are easing their way out of "mobile" and into "manufactured."

- In many parks you must buy an existing home, or a home from a manufacturer the developer prefers. You cannot bring in a unit of your own choice.

- After talking to the park owner about charges for hookup and utilities, talk to some of the residents. How *is* life there? Is there talk of the park owner's selling? This has happened in areas of the country where land is scarce and a single-family home developer has bought a chunk of real estate that has been an older, smaller mobile-home community, and unit owners have had to move their homes.

- Don't forget there may be a "no children" rule in force in the community you're considering. (See the "A Baby? Maybe" box, page 26.)

- You can check your state mobile-home association, usually located in the state capital, for the names of mobile communities in your area.

See how many housing options you have in addition to the ubiquitous condominium and resale home? There is still another coming up in the next chapter, for those who see their homes as perhaps even more of a personal statement than most.

ARE YOU ON THE SAME WAVELENGTH ABOUT
THE TYPE OF HOME YOU ARE CONSIDERING?

	YOU	HIM
Is this choice being made for financial reasons only?		
Do you feel he/she is being pressured into this choice by family or friends?		
What does he/she want in this home that doesn't really matter to you?		
Do you think what he/she wants is realistic for this time of your lives?		
Do you worry about this particular housing choice (understanding its complexities; too much maintenance; etc.)?		
How long, realistically, do you think you will stay in this place?		
If you had your choice (probable translation: a fatter savings account), what type of home would you choose?		

11

BUILDING
A HOUSE
YOURSELVES

Why a special mention of this subject, when other housing choices were grouped together in the preceding chapter?

Because building their own home is a dream of many Americans, whatever their age or the amount in their savings account. A couple approaching retirement age may choose to build a bungalow in a warm climate. Perhaps the would-be builders have a growing family, and envision finally having enough space—and the layout of their choice—in a home they want to construct themselves. Or the couple may be newly married, and after hours of discussing the house they want, and dismissing the ones they've seen for sale, ask, "Why not build one ourselves?"

Do you fit into this last category and have a strong desire to build your own place? Or is it *his* dream, while you have doubts about your ability to undertake this ultimate do-it-yourself project? If the latter, the news is good. You can almost certainly build a house yourself, even if you hardly know a 2 × 4 from an 8½ × 11. Even if *he* doesn't, either. Of course, building it yourself does not mean hammering in every nail. In almost all instances, novices call in professionals for many of the tougher jobs. They will feel more comfortable with painting, putting up cabinets, constructing a deck, and so forth. Of course, if either of you has building skills, then your involvement with the project will be a good deal more hands-on than the typical beginner's.

Nearly one out of three new houses is *not* constructed in a subdivision, and half of the nontract homes are owner-built. The builders aren't all skilled in the construction trades. Here is how they do it.

Factory-Built Houses

These are houses assembled in a plant and shipped to the building site. Some go out in thousands of pieces, others in whole panels or halves of houses. This is opposed to the traditional method of building a house from basement to roof right on the lot. These homes can roughly be divided into (1) modular homes, where the house is delivered in complete rooms or groups of rooms, which are hoisted into place with a crane and then fastened together; (2) the panelized house, where the floor and wall sections are sent from the factory, then erected at the site so that the builder-owner or a contractor can work on finishing the interior at his or her own pace; and (3) kit houses, where the manufacturer sends out everything needed to put the house together, from boards to nails—even, sometimes to kitchen appliances, wet bars, and fireplaces. There can be thousands of pieces shipped to form a kit home. Directions for assembly are included, of course. Yes, it all sounds like playing with Lincoln Logs, and that is exactly what it is, on an *extremely* large scale.

All of these houses are shipped from the manufacturer by train, if you live some distance away, and then transferred to a flatbed truck for delivery to your building site.

There is nothing second-rate about factory-built homes, if they are purchased from the right manufacturer. Indeed, many homes around the country built in subdivisions and carrying high price tags are assembled at the building site. They can be somewhat less expensive than conventionally built houses, although the costs of the factory-made variety can also rise well into six figures.

Virtually every architectural style is available. Victorians, Cape Cods, A-frames, ranches, colonials—all can be rolled onto the lot where you're building. Dome houses and log cabins may be the most frequently discussed among the selection of kit houses available. If you still don't see what you want, you can present your own plans; many manufacturers will create that home for you.

Besides potential cost-saving, the beauty of factory-built housing, of course, is that one of these homes can be finished in two to five months—about half the time it takes to build a custom house on a site (that is, a modular put up by professionals).

Developers prefer modular houses. *You* are more likely to choose the kit home, which is popular with do-it-yourselfers. We will concentrate on kit purchases here. For information about finding kit manufacturers and what they offer, contact the National Association of Home Builders, 15th and M Streets NW, Washington, D.C. 20005.

WHAT WILL A KIT HOME COST?

Prices depend on the size and style of the house, and what comes with the kit itself. Some kits are quite complete, while others basically consist of just a frame. So it's difficult to estimate what yours might cost. The base price for most kits runs from around $12,000 to $50,000, which includes precut exterior walls, a roof and insulation, subfloor, windows, exterior doors, and blueprints.

Sometimes you can buy interior doors, flooring, appliances, cabinets, and certain extras from the manufacturer. In other instances you will have to go to outside suppliers. (Land is not included in these prices, of course, but will be discussed later in this chapter.)

Very broadly speaking, your finished home will cost about three times the price of the kit, not including land and any special interior finishes you might choose.

Where are the savings? For one thing, you are not paying an architect's fee. If you do virtually all the work yourself, you can save as much as 25 percent over traditional building costs. Even if you hire out the entire project, from a contractor to erect the house to someone to paint the interior walls, you are likely to save the approximately 3 to 8 percent a developer would make in building and selling a home.

There are other considerations, however. Let's say you want to purchase a $45,000 split-level-home kit. Is $45,000 the cost of the house? Here are some extras you may have to pay that will add to that price tag:

$ 700   clearing the site for the house
3,000   sinking a well
4,000   installing a septic system
6,000   a full basement (perhaps only $2,000 if you decide on just a foundation)
3–5,000   utility-line hookups if there are no existing utility lines on the land

What if you want upgrades to the kit package—maybe substituting better-quality siding or improved insulation? What about what the kit does not provide? What if you decide, after all, to hire a contractor? What about tools? And then there's the heating system, the plumbing, and electrical work, which, unless you are professionally licensed, you may not want to do yourselves— and indeed could be prohibited from doing by local laws—and so must farm out?

You can see that your $45,000 home can become quite a bit more costly. Perhaps that will not matter to you. You are looking for the experience of homebuilding, or you want a home that can be erected in just a small percentage of the time it takes for one of conventional construction to be completed. Maybe cost overruns will not seriously affect your budget.

If you are building it yourselves to save money, however, the bottom line is that you must do much or most of the work yourselves. Only "sweat equity" will hold down the cost. You will need friends to help you regularly, and you will need Uncle Fred, the electrician, to volunteer to wire the house, and your husband's buddy Bert to offer to put in the foundation, and so forth. At the very least, if you do hire a contractor, have him leave a good part of the interior unfinished so that you can complete it yourselves. This will mean some savings.

PAYING FOR A KIT HOME

Manufacturers usually ask for a down payment of 10 to 25 percent of the cost of a package at the time an order is placed. The balance is paid COD. Companies differ, however, and some may break the payments into three stages, although the balance still falls due on delivery. Very rarely, deliveries will be made if the owner-builder merely shows a commitment letter from a lender so the company knows the money is on the way. But don't count on that strategy.

Once you've made your down payment to the kit company, where do you get the money to pay for the kit, and the work that goes with putting up your house? First, talk to the manufacturer. Many of them direct clients to financing sources. Some also offer services that allow you to buy the initial shell, so that when you approach a lender for a bank loan to complete the house, the project is at least off the ground (literally!). Weigh all of the terms carefully, of course.

For the most part, you can expect to apply for a construction loan that eventually leads to a permanent mortgage. You can secure a construction loan from one lender, and then shop at other banks for the mortgage. Or you can go for a "combo loan" from the same lender. With the combo loan you are usually given the lender's version of an option on a permanent mortgage, so that you can—and should—shop around to see if other institutions offer better terms when it comes time to converting the loan to a mortgage.

The application is the same as for any mortgage (see Chapter 15). But the lender is going to take a look at *you* in this instance, too. *Can* you both build a house? You will need to bring with you a set of blueprints, specifications of all materials used in the house (provided by the manufacturer), a detailed work-up of all costs, and a copy of the deed to the land.

It pays to dress in a businesslike manner, and bring all that documentation in an attaché case or portfolio. You want to reassure the lender that his investment will be safe. If you have no construction experience, the lender may ask you to hire a general contractor before approving the loan. If you have attended one of the nation's owner-builder schools (see below), bring documentation; it may help show your seriousness of purpose and some aptitude. Owning your lot outright is also considered an asset, of course. What the lender is trying to avoid is giving good money toward construction of a house that may never be completed, or may be done in so slipshod a manner that it is virtually unsalable in the event the bank should have to foreclose on it.

The construction loan money will be released in stages, to allow you to pay for work as it progresses. When the house is finished, and the lender considers it satisfactory, you will be granted a permanent, long-term mortgage just like everybody else's.

It may take a while to secure this type of financing, although you may have little trouble in the West and Midwest, where stalwart build-it-yourself types are more common. But if you take note of these suggestions, you are not likely to fail even in the effete East.

CAN YOU BUILD A HOUSE YOURSELF?

You probably can. As stated above, kit homes come with detailed instructions, and many manufacturers will send an on-site person to assist you at a daily fee of $100 or so. You may want to call in a contractor to "frame up" the place, and then take it from there yourselves. Read all you can on the subject of do-it-yourself homebuilding. Ask questions of the manufacturer or his representative.

Ronnie and Carl built their own home in a small southern community, thanks to a wedding gift of a half acre of land from Ronnie's folks. They ordered a three-bedroom, one-story ranch kit, which cost $20,000 and included exterior and interior walls,

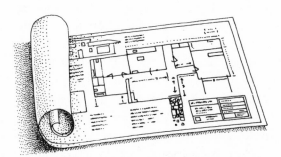

doors, plywood for roofing, and all the necessary nails. "We could have bought a more complete unit," Ronnie recalls, "but we bought more of a shell so we could do some work ourselves. And this was affordable for us." The two subcontracted the plumbing, foundation, heating, air-conditioning, and electrical work. They paid the $20,000 out of savings, and applied for a $50,000 construction loan (which later became a mortgage) to finish the house.

Friends helped a lot, and so did both sets of parents. Ronnie and Carl both hold office jobs and had only weekends to work on the house. The site was just seven miles from their apartment, though, and so eventually, once the work became just painting, putting up doors and cabinets, and similar interior jobs, they headed for the house in the evening after work, too. In all, it took seven months. This is, by and large, how most inexperienced do-it-yourselfers handle building their homes.

How long is building a house likely to take *you?* That depends. If you have only weekends, and have two or three friends to help you, you might be able to finish a kit home in a little over a year. Working full-time on the house and hiring electricians, plumbers, and a few other professionals, you may be able to move in after four months. One consideration that enters into this, of course, is how far you live from the building site. Another is how many friends will help you, and how often.

One way of preparing yourselves for this adventure is by taking a course. . . .

Owner-Builder Schools

These became popular in the 1970s as part of the back-to-the-land movement: build your own house, grow your own food, become self-sufficient. Today, there are dozens of owner-builder schools around the country. The first was Shelter Institute in Bath, Maine, which opened its doors in 1974 and continues to offer courses and workshops year-round.

At builder schools, you can take courses in the evening, learn one phase of construction in a long weekend or take two- and three-week-long programs during the summer. Some of the teaching is done in classrooms and workshops; then students head out to a building site in the area, where a house is under construction, so that they can learn by doing.

The advantage of the schools, particularly for those who are unfamiliar with construction work, is picking up what might be badly needed self-confidence about the building project, plus some skills that will last a lifetime. Students also learn the jargon and, when they return home, are quite comfortable talking with the guys at the lumberyard, with contractors and others in the field. Building becomes demystified.

Of course, another advantage to these courses is that the certificate of completion can be added to your portfolio when you head to a mortgage lender for financing.

The cost of "tuition" at owner-builder schools varies widely, according to the school and the subject being offered. A two-week homebuilding course might cost $200 to $600 (usually there is a special combination rate for couples). Sometimes the figure includes lodging and meals, but often students are directed to homes in the area that let rooms, or to motels. Meals are extra.

For a listing of owner-builder schools around the country, send a stamped, self-addressed envelope to the magazine *Practical Homeowner,* 33 E. Minor St., Emmaus, Pa. 18049.

The Land for the House

You are not likely to consider building unless you already own the land or can buy it relatively inexpensively. In some parts of the country, buying a chunk of God's green earth is prohibitively expensive. If you can manage the lot, you may be unable to afford to put more than a birdhouse on it. So land is, quite naturally, a prime consideration. Perhaps you have been as fortunate as Ronnie and Carl, who were presented with a half acre as a wedding gift.

Or maybe you are as lucky as Carol and Ed, who were able to build a home in the expensive New York metropolitan area, even though they were only engaged and twenty-three years old. The house was completed a month before the wedding. Their good fortune came about because Ed's parents bought a little fixer-upper on a two-acre lot as an investment. They were going to redo the place and then sell it—at a profit they hoped. The older couple were able to secure a zoning variance that would

SHOULD YOU?

- Do you *both* want to do this?

- Think about stress. Does one of you feel that a new marriage, two careers, and possibly a new home or apartment is enough strain right now without taking on building a house? Be honest. If one of you is unenthusiastic, that lack of concern, disinterest, or downright hostility toward the project will only grow as the inevitable pressures of homebuilding set in and increase.

- Do you have a reliable pool of workers among relatives or friends, or do you see them distancing themselves from the project as you talk about it? If it's just going to be the two of you, plus any subcontractors you hire, allow for stretching out the completion date over several more months.

- Have you worked the numbers carefully and are you sure you're not in danger of going out on a limb financially?

- Have you assumed that building a house is going to cost you more than you anticipated and will take longer than you had thought? It's a correct assump-

tion. Will all of that cause problems?

- Are you being realistic, or too enthusiastic, about homebuilding? Do you weigh ninety-eight pounds? Are you allergic to sawdust? Do you find you're taking more and more work home in the evening and are increasingly seeing weekends jammed up, too? If none of this bothers you, you're being starry-eyed about building. Are you both planning a log home? Have you considered lifting those logs, which weigh hundreds of pounds apiece? Bricks you can do alone; logs will take help from friends.

- Have you considered the resale value of the home you are planning? Your home should fit into the neighborhood and landscape, and should be in the same price range as the others. Your style may be unique, but when it comes time to sell, that house may sit on the market for years if it is too outré. This happens sometimes with homes architects design for themselves. Exciting statements they may be, but not everyone wants to own them.

split that two-acre lot into two parcels of one acre each. The fixer-upper was one piece, and the newly created lot was given to the engaged couple, who promptly had a modular home installed on it.

If you are going to look for land, here are some points to keep in mind as you examine expanses of grass and weeds and mud:

- Never, *never* buy land sight unseen.

- Be sure local zoning laws allow you to build a house there.

- Is this land regularly hit by flash floods? Is it too rocky to build on?

- A simple point, but does it have access to a road? Selling landlocked parcels is illegal in many states. If you are considering a kit home, will the trucks be able to navigate the road(s) to your site? These are tractor-trailers forty-five to sixty-five feet long. If they can't, they will leave materials as close as possible, and then *you* will have to lug them to the construction site.

- What is around the site you are considering? Is there too much commercial construction, which may make your home less valuable in the future? An attractive green beltway, likely to be there forever? Have there been environmental laws passed protecting the forest behind your site? Visit the municipal building for a look at the master plan to be sure a toxic dump won't appear next door in a year's time.

- What's *under* the land? Getting water—and getting rid of it—might be a problem. If your area has city water, you're okay. If you are buying an individual lot, you can make the purchase subject to being assured of adequate well water. Also common are purchase contracts subject to a percolation test. This is a means of testing the soil to discover its absorbent qualities for drainage and septic-tank purposes. The better the drainage, the more expensive the land.

- The more road frontage on an already completed thorough-fare, the more valuable the piece of land. But remember, peculiarly shaped parcels—a triangle, say—may be a problem come resale time.

- Most sales of land are for cash only. The most common means of financing, when it is possible, is for the seller to hold a short-term mortgage. In certain economic situations, you may be able to buy through an installment land-purchase contract, whereby you agree to pay the seller over a certain period of time. The title does not pass to you, however, until you have made all payments, or at least a considerable number of them.

- If you are planning to buy a parcel of land on which to build a home someday—you are not sure how many years from now—remember that land is not an investment. Vacant land produces no income, and you will still have to pay real estate taxes on it, plus interest if you have financed the purchase.

YOUR MUNICIPALITY HAS AN INTEREST IN THIS, TOO

Your house will have to meet building code requirements of the community in which it is situated. To get a building permit, you will have to have your plans approved by an arm of the local government, and construction will have to pass inspection by a municipal building inspector. All of this can cause delays, so allow for them as you budget time.

There are no tax deductions for land. If you have paid cash, you will be losing interest on money that could have been placed in an income-producing investment. So unless the parcel is outstanding, from the point of view of location and for price, it would be wiser to buy when you are closer to the time of building.

Obviously, building it yourselves is not the simplest way to become homeowners. Still, those who have completed their project say the satisfaction and pride in their home has been worth the hard work. (They almost all say that once is enough, too!)

12

⁕

HOW TO
FIND
THE HOME
FOR YOU

Y ou want to be organized about this. In the past you spent the occasional Sunday or your day off driving around looking at homes open to view or just checking out neighborhoods you both found appealing. But now that you are seriously ready to buy, you realize there must be a system to this househunt game.

You're right, there is. Running helter-skelter to an open house two towns over, then driving forty miles to a new development opening, then calling to respond to a newspaper advertisement yields nothing but increased confusion and fatigue.

Here's how to househunt without tears.

NARROWING DOWN THE LOCALE

Are you going to look in the town where you are currently living? In the country? Are you going farther afield than that? By now you should know approximately, give or take a few communities, where you will confine your hunt. (If you are in the city, searching for a home in the suburbs or the country will probably require renting a car some weekends, if you don't already have one. If you're *sure* you'll be buying out of town, you may want to *buy* a car at this time.) If you work in Big City, and Towns A, B, and C are bedroom communities ringing it, those may be your choices. You are probably confining yourselves to them for one or more of the following reasons:

- You like the housing stock and the homes are within your price range.

- Commuting to your jobs is convenient and not outrageously expensive.

- Property taxes are reasonable, too.

- Services, such as shopping and banking, are handy—if not within walking distance, at least a short hop away by car.

- You are planning to have a child while living in this house, have inquired about the school system and found it is good; you note there are other children around, and maybe even community-sponsored social activities for kids.

- Speaking of children, you are looking into day care. If there is no day-care center nearby, what about the availability of women in the community who baby-sit in their homes? Are you looking at a town, or development, full of women who leave for jobs every morning? Where is day care to be found, then? If nowhere in that town, you may want to reconsider buying there.

- Maybe you've already mentally chosen one town over another because you love the big old homes there, and the sort of Tudor-style downtown strip, or perhaps your closest friend lives there. All emotional reasons, but if the reasons for buying there make budgetary sense as well, then emotion is fine. After all, even if you don't fall in love with the town and the house, you should at least like them fairly well. You don't want to spend a year or more anyplace you hate!

LOCATION

Here come those three vitally important words again: "location," "location," "location." While you'll avoid buying a home that is at the end of an airport runway, look out for other locations that may well get in your way when you plan to sell, either causing your house to remain on the market longer, or forcing you to accept a price lower than you want—those might be next to a retail or commercial building, or fronting on a busy highway.

Unusually shaped lots can be a problem, come resale time—those shaped like triangles or some other offbeat configuration. Houses built on steep slopes or those built below the level of the land are often hard to sell, too.

If you're buying into a new development, what's under the surface mud is extremely important. Poor drainage can present a daily problem. If your house is built on rock it is not likely to settle much, but if plunked on landfill it may settle unevenly. Poke around the town building inspector's office or tax assessor's office to see if a percolation test has been made and recorded on that development. In a "perc test," a hole is dug on the property, water poured in, and the rate of absorption noted. Sometimes notes are made on the composition of the earth—clay, gravel, shale—to the bottom of the hole.

What about radon, the natural gas now being found under houses in certain parts of the country? Your agent can show you proof that radon tests have been taken in the house that interests you. If there has been no test, you can request that one be made, at your expense. (In sections of the country where radon levels are significant, some sellers will have this information available for prospective buyers.)

While you are at town hall, ask to see a floodplain map, which is made by the U.S. government for many communities. No doubt you will have heard of any periodic flooding problems that may exist in the community you are considering. If they do, you will want to avoid buying land at the low point of the town or neighborhood.

As you narrow down your choice, remember that a stream in the backyard can be a detriment because of the chance of flooding, or as a risk to small children, and corner lots are often not desirable in residential real estate: too open to view, and possibly easier theft targets than houses with neighbors on both sides—too much maintenance for some buyers, too.

If you're househunting in the suburbs or the country, it's pretty simple to get a correct reading of that community or area as you drive through—attractive homes, well-kept streets, reasonably quiet—if it looks good, it probably is. For more in-depth information, you can look at a copy of the master plan for the area,

A HOME BUSINESS?

If you or your husband already runs a business from home, you know what to look for when house-hunting. But if this kind of entrepreneurship is still only in your mind, or his, you should know that some home-based businesses may be banned by local zoning laws, or you may have to apply for a variance. Talk to the real estate agent about your plans. Some houses, or neighborhoods, may just not do.

if there is one, at the Municipal or County Building, to see if and where new development is planned and how it is likely to affect the community and its property values (Is a nuclear power plant on the drawing board? Is there a protective greenbelt around the town, or certain parts of it, that will prohibit new growth?). However, looking for a home in an urban area can be different as far as appearance goes.

Maybe you know exactly where you will look in the city you have chosen. Perhaps you both work in town and know it well, block by block. But maybe you don't. You may be looking for an affordable house in town and have only heard of the truly posh neighborhoods. Everything else within the city limits is a frightening question mark to you. You can recognize slums when you see them, but what about the neighborhoods that are sort of in-between? Can they be a good buy?

Choosing a city neighborhood can be tricky. The ones you are likely to be interested in are:

1. Those that have been high-priced, with fancy addresses, for many years: Washington, D.C.'s, Georgetown and New York's Brooklyn Heights are two prime examples.

2. Ones that have been stable for years and have not attracted much press attention. These are usually heavily ethnic, with little turnover in housing stock. When homes *are* sold, they frequently go to those who already live there, particularly newly married children who want to stay near family and friends. These towns or neighborhoods can be excellent buys—good places to live, with congenial residents and property values that never drop because the blocks are well maintained and the homes in continual demand.

3. Neighborhoods that are undergoing a renaissance. You can learn more about these by reading the real estate *news* (not advertising) sections of your local paper and attending house tours, where new homeowners show off their handsomely restored houses. The tours are an excellent way of getting a feel for a community, and you can ask questions of the host and hostess in each home. They are usually quite open in talking about prices, cost of renovation, safety in the community, state of the schools, and any other concerns you may have.

These neighborhoods can be recognized by such outward signs of revival as—flower pots on house stoops, a block or neighborhood association, frequent activities and fund-raisers (like house tours), a few shops or trendy bars opening there or on the periphery of the neighborhood. Be sure you choose a neighborhood that is on the way back, not one continuing a downward slide. The latter shows *no* signs of revival. Also, folks in enclaves on the upswing can point you toward other blocks or neighborhoods in your city where buying a home is considered a safe and wise investment.

The Real Estate Agent

By all means, utilize the services of real estate agents. You may need one for each community in which you are interested. You pay no fee for an agent's services; he or she earns a commission from the seller of the house.

Finding the right agent may take a little time. You want someone with whom you feel comfortable, of course, and someone who is not turned off when you mention your price range. Be sure to select an agent who works at the job full-time, too. Part-timers, by virtue of their limited hours, are, all too often, not on top of the latest news and listings in that office and town.

How to find the good ones? Ask for names of agents from friends and co-workers who have recently purchased homes. Ask questions of the agent on duty at open houses you attend. Perhaps you and that agent will click. Again, read the real estate stories in local papers, in which agents are often mentioned by name. You can also call one or several of such national franchises as Century 21 and Gallery of Homes. They will put you in touch with an agent in the area that interests you, and you can evaluate that person yourself. You can answer newspaper advertisements of houses for sale to find an agent, but real estate offices usually assign their sales staff a certain amount of "floor time," when they must be on hand to answer blind telephone calls. You may draw someone you like or, then again, you may not. If you are inquiring about a specific house in an ad that lists the agent's name, that's different. That agent will at least be familiar with the property that interests you.

Every real estate agent will have material in his or her office about loan qualifications for homebuyers. Don't withhold information about your income or your long-term debts. You need to know just how much house you can afford, and the agent does not want to waste time showing you $250,000 houses when you are more in the $180,000 category. That's why he or she will ask your price range, or help you to determine it with questions about your income, before showing you homes. The agent will make calculations based on your responses, and come up with

WHAT TO LOOK FOR
IN A REAL ESTATE LISTING

Real estate offices keep their listings of homes for sale in a book in which one house may appear on each page. There is a picture of the home, plus details about exterior construction materials; a listing of all rooms, with their dimensions; how the house is heated; whether there is a garage or other buildings on the property; and incidentals such as recessed lighting, window shutters, wall-to-wall carpeting, ceiling moldings, and the like.

Some points to give your special attention:

- **Asking price, of course**

- **The age of the house**

- **The amount of property (dimensions of the lot)**

- **Taxes and tax rate**

- **Assessed value for tax purposes (how does this home's assessment compare with those for other properties in the area?)**

- **What is included and not included in the sale? (If furnishings that interest you do not go with the home, try to negotiate for their inclusion. If you are not successful with that strategy, you may be able to purchase them from the owner.)**

- **How long has this house been on the market? The listing date will tell you.**

a figure for a monthly mortgage payment that you will be able to carry.

He or she will also be able to provide you with information about the neighborhood or town you are considering—taxes, recreation, services, and so forth. Ask for a street map.

Many, if not most, real estate offices belong to a multiple listing service, which shows virtually every property for sale in a region, with pictures and all pertinent information available. If you work with an agent who belongs to such a service, your househunt can be less tiring. Just ask to see the listing book and page through the offerings until you see a few that catch your eye. Ask to see the "comparables book," too, which lists houses comparable to the ones that interest you and what they have sold for—asking price and selling price—within the year. That will help you avoid overpaying for a home.

Listing books can save you enormous amounts of time but, naturally, there comes a time when you have to get out of the real estate office and start going through homes.

Some tips here:

- Do only one town a day, and try for no more than five houses during that time. More than that and confusion sets in.

- Go in the agent's car, so you can concentrate on the appearance of various neighborhoods and can ask questions of the agent.

- Visit builders' open houses by yourselves. Maybe you're not planning to buy a new home from them, but you can get an idea of prices there and compare them with what you are planning to pay for, say, a resale house. You can also pick up some ideas for appliances, decorating, landscaping, and the like.

AGENTS FOR BUYERS

When dealing with real estate agents, keep in mind that they are working for the seller of the house. That is where their commission comes from and where, ethically, their loyalty must lie. Naturally, they are interested in finding you a home, because that home will bring them a commission, but their allegiance is to the seller.

A relatively new development on the real estate scene is the agent who works for the buyer exclusively. Buyer brokerage works like this: The agent attracts a prospective client, signs a retainer agreement with the buyer, locates a house the buyer wishes to buy, and agrees to negotiate on the buyer's behalf terms of sale that will be acceptable to the buyer. For this service the agent usually charges a commission of around 3 percent of the sale price.

Right now, buyer brokerage represents an extremely small percent of the market, compared with the hundreds of thousands of real estate agents who work in the traditional way.

Walking Through Houses

Look beyond the external features that attracted you to that particular property. There are other factors that will make the house work for you, and make it salable when you decide to move. Always buy with that thought in mind—resale value.

If you think you might want to move again soon, or might be transferred in a short time, buy the home that would appeal to the greatest number of potential buyers, a trick utilized by corporate and military families who are always on the move. This means purchasing a basic house, with no extraordinary features that may keep it on the market longer than you would like—five bedrooms, for example, won't do, neither will a swimming pool (not all that popular with buyers).

Look at the traffic pattern in the house, too—another prime consideration whether you plan to stay a short time or forever. An awkward layout of rooms is also likely to be a poor buy. Going through a bedroom to get to another bedroom, for instance, is not good. Neither is difficulty in getting from the kitchen to the backyard, both for ease in outdoor entertaining and the ability to keep an eye on small children.

Does this place need only a few cosmetic improvements, like new carpeting, new lighting fixtures, maybe some paint or wallpaper? Or is a major renovation called for? If the latter, where will the rehab money come from?

Is there enough storage space? Enough bathrooms? Do you want to add a powder room to the main floor? Is there room for one?

If you think you might want to add on to the house one day—a solarium, office space for the two of you, or perhaps to start a family—is there room for expansion?

What is the state of the wiring, the heating system, the plumbing? What about the roof? Problems in these areas mean large cash outlays. They are considerations you will definitely want to know more about before you buy. So you will no doubt go for:

The House Inspection

It's wise not even to think of buying an older home (and that can be anywhere from 15 years old to 150 years) without having it looked over by an engineer or house inspector. Perhaps your Uncle Charlie knows houses like the back of his hand and will gladly come over and crawl around the house you have in mind. Or you might want to seek out a professional house inspection service. There are usually several of these in most areas, some of which are local and some nationwide companies.

A house inspector will prowl around the house you are considering and give you a detailed, typed report on the state of the major systems, walls, basement, exterior siding, and any other feature that might cause you concern—and big bucks—somewhere down the road.

You do not have to have an inspection made of every house that interests you. A house is inspected only after you make an offer on it and that offer is accepted. The contract will usually specify that the sale is contingent on (1) your being able to secure financing and (2) a house inspection (including a termite report) satisfactory to you. So wait for the inspection until you have very firmly chosen *the* house.

Inspectors charge fees ranging from $100 to $300, depending on the service and the area of the country. It's a cheap price to pay, really, for the peace of mind of knowing just what expenses are likely to lie ahead of you with this home. You should note, though, that while your Uncle Charlie may tell you whether or not you should buy this house, a professional house inspector will offer no opinion. He offers just the facts, ma'am. Some inspectors do termite inspections, others do not. You may have to call in a local exterminator for a reading on termites.

A word of caution: if possible, do not use a house inspection service recommended by your real estate agent. While these companies may be perfectly fine, large and reputable, the inspector may unconsciously feel some allegiance to the realty agency and will not report anything that might kill the sale.

You can find inspection services by asking around among friends and business associates or by contacting the American Society of Home Inspectors at 3299 K St. NW, Washington, D.C. 20007 (tel: 202-842-3096). They can send you a list of member inspectors in your area.

Do not be put off by what the inspector may find. There is no such thing as the perfect older house. Some of the problems you may well be able to live with, or to change without too much fuss or cash.

YOU WANT THE DRAPERIES? ASK FOR THEM

By all means see what is included in the sale of the resale house or condo you choose. Does it come with that refrigerator? The ceiling fixtures? The carpeting? The fireplace accessories? If you see some appliance or furnishing you'd like to have, negotiate for it to be included along with the home. Maybe the sellers are trading the house for an apartment and wouldn't mind leaving the patio furniture.

Purchase contracts usually contain the contingencies noting that the sale depends on your securing financing for the purchase, and your finding a home inspection report satisfactory, if you choose to have one. Have any other extras you want to secure for yourselves written in as well.

New Homes

There is no need to hire an inspection service if you have purchased a new home, of course. Usually new houses are protected by a builder warranty. The advantages of a new house include: brand-new construction; new appliances; more up-to-date heating and cooling systems, making them more energy efficient than older houses. On the minus side, that new construction could be shoddy; you may have a hard time getting the builder back to do minor fixing covered by your warranty; frequently you will be left to do the landscaping yourselves.

Be very sure as you go through model homes in a development that you know *exactly* what you are purchasing. The model is designed to sell the other units, and usually top-of-the line appliances and wall-to-wall carpeting are used. When it comes to buying, you may have to select less costly brand names offered by the developer because of your own budget restrictions. Did the builder add on that patio just as a marketing ploy for the development? What about the draperies? Have all of this spelled out in your purchase contract, so you will know what is standard and what you will have to pay extra for.

A good bargaining tool in a slow seller's market is to ask the builder or his agent to throw in a few extras for the sale. Maybe the draperies *aren't* ordinarily included. If you ask, you may get them—or the dishwasher or another appliance or furnishing that sweetens the sale a little for you. In times of economic concern, whether nationally or in one particular region of the country, the builder may well try to spur sales with offers of paying closing costs or $1,500 toward new furniture, or feature some other attraction. Go for as much as you can get!

Better ask, too, if you are buying into a development, whether there are monthly maintenance fees. While these assessments are routinely paid by condominium and cooperative owners, now a growing number of single-family communities have home-owners' associations that handle the upkeep of streets and side-walks. Fees can range from about $25 a year to as much as $150 or so a month.

Condo Shopping

Your prime concern when selecting a condominium—besides choosing one that is attractive and well situated—is the financial health of that community. If the place looks a little run-down, that may be because no one cares enough to have it spruced up. But it may mean there's no money for the job! Which is the truth you may learn by reading the financial statement. See if there have been any recent special assessments—new roof for the clubhouse, or repaving the parking lot, for example. You can ask members of the condo board or the management company if any major changes or repairs are being contemplated. Maybe plans for a clubhouse are on the drawing board, which may or may not interest you, but which you will certainly have to pay for if there is not enough money in the condo's reserve fund. If there is not, how much more will the community have to raise through special assessments?

If you are afraid you'll miss something by trying to plow through the financial statement yourselves, by all means engage an accountant to look it over for you. This is an important document and you will not rest easy if you are still wondering, even after you move in, what's going on in that community.

Naturally, you will also want to know the monthly maintenance fee and what that covers. You should know that in brand-new complexes, to make them more attractive and salable, the figure may be "low-balled" by the developer. If it is, it can rise dramatically after the development is turned over to the unit owners.

You may want to ask about subletting your unit, if you think that might be an issue somewhere down the road. By the same token, however, too many renters in a complex is not a good sign, and one you should watch out for. Condos are frequently purchased for investment purposes, with the buyers never living in their units. Owners make the best occupants, stabilize the community, and keep it well maintained. So before you buy, ask about absentee investors there.

Negotiating the Sale

Naturally, asking prices are not firm, and you can negotiate all you want, as long as the seller is still interested. Real estate agents are required by law to pass on every reasonable offer to the seller, and offering $20,000, or even more, below the asking price is still considered reasonable. Don't be intimidated. How long buyer and seller continue to go back and forth will depend in great measure on whether the house or condo is overpriced (you will know whether it is because you have checked "comparables," as mentioned earlier in this chapter), the state of the real estate market where you are, and the condition of the overall national economy. Is it a buyer's or a seller's market?

An important tip: never tell the real estate agent how much you're willing to pay for that house. Remember, he or she represents the seller and can always tell that individual, "Well, they'll go up to $189,000," when you have told the agent to make an initial offer of $185,000 but have indicated you would be willing to go to $189,000. Keep that top figure to yourselves, as you increase your offer, if need be, in increments of $500 or $1,000.

THE BOTTOM LINE

Your first home is just that—the start of what will probably be several houses or condominiums you will own over the course of your lifetime. It is not likely you will be able to buy the home of your dreams first time out. So try not to have too many unrealistic expectations or be disappointed in what you *do* buy. You are fortunate, in a time when first-time buyers are dwindling in number, to find it possible to buy a home at all. Congratulations on that feat. Thanks to your initial purchase, one day you will be able to trade up to a home closer to what you truly want. It *will* happen!

Most real estate agents will refuse to present a verbal offer to a seller. If they do, protect yourself. You do not want your first offer to be accepted if you would like to negotiate more. Avoid the signed contract that locks up the deal if the seller accepts your offer, even if you're pressured by the agent. Go for the "binder," a shorter offer form, which is still a written offer, including offering price, a closing date for the sale, financing information, and a list of contingencies. An earnest-money check (usually required, in an amount of 1 to 2 percent of the price of the home) is returnable if the sale does not go through.

Be sure the binder form contains a statement to the effect that the agreement is subject to a mutually acceptable contract to purchase to be drawn within three or five business days and signed by all parties involved in the transfer of the property. If you do not have that statement either already in the form or written in, that binder could turn into a legally enforceable contract. Do not take no for an answer if your agent turns aside the binder or the request for that protective clause. Those days between the time you sign the binder and the time you sign the contract give you the opportunity to consult an attorney if you wish.

Also tell the agent you do not want that earnest-money check cashed or deposited in any account until there is an agreement on price. Sometimes the return of those checks can take a while, and you may need this money to make offers on other houses.

Do You Need a Lawyer?

It would be foolish to buy a first home (perhaps even successive houses) without having a lawyer steer you through the process, which can be complicated. What if you have trouble with the seller over some point of the transaction? Do you want to learn about recording fees and surveys or let someone else think about those details? Do you want to worry until the day you close—and perhaps even thereafter—that you have missed something, that no one, aside from the inexperienced two of you, cares about your interests? Most housing transfers are without incident, but in 5 percent or so of transactions, problems develop, either before a closing or after. Attorneys' fees vary. Some charge a flat 1 percent of the sale price of the property; with others the fee is anywhere from $500 to $800, regardless of the sale price of the home. This is worth the expense when you consider that you are talking about an investment of thousands of dollars, and years and years of a mortgage commitment.

Now, about the down payment on the home you like. Some suggestions for putting together that amount of money follow in the next chapter.

WORKSHEET FOR HOUSEHUNTING

Before you start visiting houses, do some thinking about what you expect in the home you buy. Some features may jump to the head of the list, perhaps surprising one or both of you.

FEATURES	MUST HAVE	WOULD LIKE	DON'T CARE	DON'T WANT
New house				
Resale house				
Condominium				
Two bedrooms				
Three bedrooms				
Four bedrooms or more				
Two full baths				
Bath and a half				
Dining room				
Dining area				
Finished basement				
Skylight(s)				
Attractive landscaping				
Backyard				
Fireplace(s)				
Garage				

FEATURES	MUST HAVE	WOULD LIKE	DON'T CARE	DON'T WANT
Porch(es)				
Central air conditioning				
Security system				
LOCATION				
Good investment area				
Near transportation				
Near schools				
Near shopping, banks, etc.				
Near park or open land				

13

WHERE THE DOWN PAYMENT MIGHT COME FROM

Some couples wait until they think they have enough money to plunk down on a home before they go househunting; others drive around, visit open houses, and talk to real estate agents before they're sure they have enough money for a down payment, or indeed before they know how much that will be.

Who is smarter? Surprise! While there is certainly nothing foolish about waiting to look for a home until you have enough money to purchase one, it may be wise to educate yourself and talk to those in the field while you are still unsure whether your savings are adequate. Why? Because there are programs that can make a homeowner out of you even if you have only a minimal amount for a down payment. Of course, you have to be able to qualify for a mortgage (more about that in Chapter 15), and that means having an income sufficient to carry those monthly charges. But if it is only the down payment that is holding you up, read on.

How Much? How Little?

Broadly speaking, you will need 10 to 20 percent of the purchase price of a house as a down payment. The amount needed may fall at the lower end of that range, where builders are selling homes and offering low rates (some may drop to 5 percent, although that is not happening as often as it used to), and sometimes in a sluggish real estate market, where buyers are welcomed by lenders with open arms and application blanks.

At the higher end—the more common requirement—are those who are young, who have little work experience, or whose income is not very grand. Occasionally 25 percent will be required for applicants with a problem credit record. You may want to *offer* 25 percent, which can get you a mortgage with low documentation requirements (no checking your income). These are known as "low-doc" loans.

"Leverage" has always been a key term in real estate; it means buying the most you can with the smallest investment of your own money. Applied to a home, it can mean being able to pay $15,000 down and getting in return a $150,000 house.

But the last several years have brought serious changes to the homebuying market in the area of down payments. Mortgage lenders were stung by the recession of the early 1980s, when many homebuyers walked away from their properties, leaving behind houses on which lenders had to foreclose. But the lenders did not want those houses either, and could resell only with great difficulty and at a great cost to them. Homeowners walked because their investments were minimal, perhaps a 5 percent down payment. Today, lenders are determined those dark days will not be repeated. Now, they say, owners will think twice before abandoning their commitments, because now they will have more invested in their houses. So down payments have risen to the point where more than half today's homebuyers pay 20 percent.

What if you see just the home for you, one with monthly mortgage payments you can comfortably afford, but you're shy the $14,000 down payment required by the lender? You have only $9,000. What can you do?

(An important note here: If you're really counting the pennies and have a goal in mind for a down payment, don't forget you will also have to have money for closing costs on that home. These run 3 to 5 percent of the cost of the mortgage, and are payable before you are given the keys to the house or condo you buy. So maybe a down payment isn't all you need. . . .)

Some Sources of Help

Consider these possibilities if you need to find assistance in putting together a down payment:

- Can you ask your parents or his for the amount you still need? Doing this can make sense: while you are laboriously saving, the cost of houses continues to rise. You may never catch up. Of course, the folks should be in good financial shape or they should not even be approached.

  Lenders frown on applicants who borrow money for a down payment. They will require what is known as a "gift letter" from the donor stating that this is money being given, not lent, and that no repayment is expected. You will need copies of that letter to take with you in making a mortgage application.

  The simplest form of help is an outright *gift of some or all of the down payment.* The Internal Revenue Service allows an individual to give up to $10,000 per person per year tax-free. A married couple can give a child $20,000 and, if the child is married, another $20,000 to the child's spouse, making a total of $40,000.

  However the folks plan to handle helping you in this manner, they should first consult their accountant to be sure the way they have chosen is the most beneficial to them.

- One fairly common form of assistance in helping first-time buyers get a toehold on the homeownership ladder is *private mortgage insurance (PMI).* This is a policy offered by several companies nationwide that allows buyers to make down payments of only 10 percent or less on a home. They are charged a fraction of a percent of the amount of the mortgage as an annual premium. The insurance can be dropped at a point when the lender feels its investment is safe, usually after five to seven years. This is a policy real estate agents can help you secure.

Lenders usually require PMI of borrowers who need 95 percent financing on their homes, but, sadly, insurers have been tightening their standards for offering that coverage. Borrowers usually must have a good credit history to secure a policy. The premium is up to 1 percent of the mortgage at closing, with annual premiums thereafter from around 0.35 to 0.5 percent of the mortgage.

- *Loans backed by the federal government* are another source of assistance. Those loans insured by the Federal Housing Administration (FHA) call for 5 percent down payments, with an insurance policy you will have to pay up front at the closing, not spread out in monthly premiums. It, too, represents a small percentage of the loan. Loans that are backed by the Veterans Administration (VA) require *no* down payment and no insurance. Anyone can apply for an FHA-backed loan; veterans or widows of veterans who died of service-related injuries qualify for VA-insured loans.

  If you are interested in buying in a rural area, you might investigate the Farmers Home Administration (FmHA), which also offers lower-than-market down payment requirements and interest rates. There are some restrictions here—one is that this must be a principal residence, not a second home—but if you qualify, the terms can be excellent.

- Every state but Kansas offers a *state-sponsored low-cost homebuying program*. Down payments are usually around 5 percent. When mortgage interest rates hit, say, 10 percent on the open market, homes under this program can cost owners an interest rate of just 8 percent of purchase price.

Have you ever seen on a local news program a segment showing young people lined up in front of a bank or other lending institution, sometimes with folding chairs, prepared to stay overnight in the spot they have captured? These are the programs for which they are waiting to apply. Money, obtained from bond issues, disappears quickly here, usually going to waiting applicants the first day its availability is announced. The programs are operated through a state's Mortgage Finance Agency or Housing and Mortgage Finance Agency.

You will find some restrictions. There are income ceilings, but they are not inordinately low. Househunters must usually be first-time buyers. Eligible homes are within predetermined boundaries, generally neighborhoods in need of economic boosting. Still, thousands of young people have become homeowners over the last decade or so thanks to these programs. They are always in danger of disappearing because of budget cuts, however, so even as you read this they may be part of history. Call your state governor's office for more information.

- Next comes *"equity sharing."* This is relatively new to the residential real estate scene, although it has been used to cement commercial deals for many years. And of course it has long been an informal means of family assistance, usually with the older generation helping the younger.

Let's say your husband's folks (known as the "owner-investors" here) put up the down payment you need. In return, they become co-owners of the house with you (you are the "owner-occupants"). All of your names appear on the deed. For them to take advantage of certain tax benefits, you must pay them a fair market rent (no token amounts allowed) for the half of the house that you are inhabiting. The folks come in for some nice tax advantages, including those afforded landlords. You get the ordinary homeowner tax deductions—mortgage interest and real estate taxes—but only for one-half of the home. A contract is drawn up by the attorney representing any one of you, setting forth when you can buy out their share if you like, what happens if one side wants to sell the house, and so forth. When it *is* sold, profits are split in the same ratio as ownership.

There are several equity sharing companies around the country that match would-be homeowners with investors who want to put their money somewhere but do not want a hands-on investment. Most of these companies operate only within their state or region of the country. A real estate agent can tell you if there is a company near you. An equity-sharing company can help even if you already have owner-investors, in your parents or his, since they also offer assistance in the particulars a contract between the two couples should contain.

Equity sharing works with strangers being matched; it should certainly be profitable, financially and otherwise, when the commitment is all in the family.

- Another way around a lack of up-front cash might be for one set of *parents to co-sign for a home you buy,* perhaps making the down payment as well. This is done occasionally if the househunters are very young or have not yet established careers. You won't want to involve the folks in this situation, of course, if there is any chance you will not be able to keep up the mortgage payments. They are, after all, responsible for that loan. Parents contemplating co-signing should consider their own needs, too. Borrowers are usually expected to disclose the co-sign agreement if they apply for any new loan. You may be refused credit if your potential debt is considered excessive, even though you and your husband have been making mortgage payments faithfully.

Only a lender can cancel a co-sign agreement. If the two of you, after a few years with such a mortgage, have a substantial increase in earnings, the parents may ask the lending institution holding the mortgage to be released from their liability. Lenders may say yes, but since it is to their advantage to keep a co-signer, it isn't guaranteed.

- Perhaps the *seller of the home could lend you the money* you still need. This is likely to work only in a very slow seller's market, however, or when the seller is extremely eager to unload his or her property. Perhaps the couple who own the house that interests you are eager to sell and move into the home they have just purchased in Florida. They may well agree to help you, in return for your taking that house off their hands.

- Another strategy that works, for the most part, only in a stagnant market, is the *lease/purchase option.* Here, you rent a house, signing a contract that states that at the end of a year (or two) you will be allowed to buy it. Some or all of your rent might be applied to the purchase, making the acquisition of a down payment nearly painless.

- Finally, *call your area office of the U.S. Department of Housing and Urban Development (HUD)* (listed in the telephone book under U.S. Government). Sometimes there are regional, or local, housing programs with funds earmarked for house-hunters in a small target area. You may qualify for down-payment assistance under a program in your very own town, a program whose existence may come as a complete surprise to you.

Feel better about that elusive amount of money you need, now that you have so many options? Coming up: the second and third stages of the financial side of the homebuying process—going for a mortgage and closing on the home you have chosen. But first, a side trip through the world of insurance.

14

A FEW WORDS ABOUT HOMEOWNER'S INSURANCE

Y ou will want a homeowner's insurance policy for the protection of your house. Mortgage lenders insist buyers purchase such a policy for the safety of *their* investment in the event the house is damaged or destroyed. Lenders have a few minimum requirements for coverage—usually the insurance must cover at least the amount of the loan; some lenders make higher demands. Beyond that, it is up to you to decide how much protection you want. Insurance is discussed now since you will want to look over coverage available as you go through the homebuying process. At the closing on your home, you will have to show proof that you have taken out a homeowner's policy, and have paid the first premium, if that is a requirement of the lender.

You can shop at various agencies, but the real estate salesperson who sold you your home might direct you to a carrier, too, often the insurance arm of her own realty firm. That's fine, but check out other insurers as well.

You will learn that in this field an insurance "agent" is a representative of a specific insurance company, while a "broker" sells insurance for several companies.

The *basic* homeowner's policy protects your home, shrubs, trees, and outside structures from eleven perils, including fire, theft, vandalism, lightning, and windstorms. The *broad* policy adds another seven items, including protection against damage from frozen pipes, falling objects, and sprinkler systems.

You are covered only for the misfortunes listed on your policy, which is why it is important to read that document carefully before signing it.

The standard homeowner's policy consists of coverage for 100 percent of the *replacement value of your home* (80 percent is the minimum to consider), plus coverage for your *personal belongings* and *liability coverage* to protect you if someone is injured in your home or on your property. "Replacement value" is not market value. It is the amount you'd need to rebuild your home if that should ever become necessary. "Market value" is the price your home would bring if you sold it today, a figure for which insurers will not offer coverage since, for one thing, it includes land, which is uninsurable.

If you are uncertain about what the replacement cost of your home would be, you can call in a real estate appraiser or ask your insurance agent or broker.

Your personal belongings are insured for cash value, which is replacement cost less depreciation. The usual coverage for the contents of a home is 50 percent of the home's insured value. So a house carrying $100,000 worth of insurance will be covered by $50,000 for personal property. Some companies now offer full replacement cost coverage on personal belongings.

Regarding personal liability coverage, the average verdict award for something as relatively minor as a knee injury is now around $300,000. And that's not the worst that could happen to a guest on your property. The $100,000 liability limit, so common for years, is now being increased. You will probably find that for as little as an additional $20 a year in premium costs you can raise that protection to $300,000 per incident, a figure now considered adequate.

You might also give some thought to "umbrella coverage," liability protection that picks up where both your homeowner's and automobile policies leave off. Umbrellas can cost around $150 for $1 million worth of coverage, going up to $250 to $300 for as much as $10 million. By all means look into this if your life situation presents certain opportunities for injury. Do you have a swimming pool, for instance, or three German shepherds? Does a visitor have to climb thirty-nine steps to get to your cliffside house? Do you do extensive volunteer work, and are not insured by the group(s) for which you work? Do you give many parties? A growing number of states have laws holding sellers or servers of alcoholic beverages liable, at least in part, for a customer's or guest's actions while under the influence of alcohol after they leave the seller or server's premises.

As you may have noticed, this has become a highly litigious society, where friends and neighbors sue at a snap of the fingers. And not just for payment of medical bills, either, but for full-range compensation. This could mean that if a twenty-two-year-old ballerina slips on your icy steps, ruining her promising career, she may well want to take you to court for more than just medical expenses.

While you may never need liability protection, it is nice to know it's there—and in a sufficient amount.

There are many variations on the homeowner's package and limits to certain categories of coverage. Investigate them all. Given the variables of how much the carrier you select charges, how much you are insuring your home for, the amount of liability coverage you want, and any special protection you are seeking, you may pay anywhere from a few hundred dollars to over $1,000 annually in premiums.

The standard deductible is often $100. You can save 10 to 35 percent in premiums if you elect higher deductibles, the highest being around $1,000. Remember, the purpose of this coverage is to protect you from a wipeout of thousands, perhaps hundreds of thousands, of dollars. You may well be able to afford to pay out $1,000 before the insurance company picks up the rest.

You are not likely to have your premiums increase after you have filed a claim, although depending on the amount of the claim(s), and their frequency, a company may decide not to renew your coverage.

The Fair Access to Insurance Requirements (FAIR) plan is in effect in more than 20 states, offering insurance to those who have difficulty securing protection for a high-risk property or one situated in a high-risk area. Your real estate agent can tell you more about FAIR.

Special Endorsements

Do you have special treasures you want protected? Most policies will cover up to, say, $1,000 for loss of jewelry, furs, and watches, and up to $2,500 for silverware (figures vary from one carrier to another and according to coverage purchased). But there is often no provision for such special items as antiques, art, and valuable collectibles. They can be covered with the purchase of a personal-articles *floater,* at an additional cost to you. Coverage applies whether or not the articles are in your home at the time of loss. It also includes damage or breakage, which is not covered by the standard homeowner's policy.

Do you feel your house is worth more than the amount an insurer is willing to cover? Occasionally owners claim they have put in thousands of dollars in renovation, or that certain features of the house, built in when it was constructed perhaps more than one hundred years ago, cannot be duplicated today. It may even be a designated regional or state landmark. Replacement cost, using modern materials, cannot bring that house back to its original state. If you find yourself in this position, first have the house appraised professionally before you approach an insurance agent or broker. You will probably have to shop around quite a bit for such a policy. Insurers are wary of coverage above replacement value because of the fear of arson for profit. Still, finding the right coverage is not an impossibility.

Other Protections

Nowadays you can find insurance coverage for practically every calamity that may befall your home except nuclear wipeout. Here are two specialties that are most common.

FLOOD AND EARTHQUAKE

Fire protection goes along with a standard homeowner's policy, but coverage for these two calamities does not. Earthquake insurance is a separate provision, costing perhaps $150 to $200 or so in annual premiums. The average homeowner's policy also does not provide coverage for damage from floods or mud slides—which sometimes comes as a surprise to those hit by those acts of nature. These, too, will require separate coverage.

In fact, your lender may demand flood insurance if you live in a problem area, which is usually designated as such by a federal, state, or local assessment of the region. If you are buying in a flood-prone region, you might call 1-800-638-6620 to see if your community is eligible for coverage under the low-cost National Flood Insurance Program (NFIP). Your insurance agent or broker will also know about this.

There is another coverage that has been touted in recent years.

MORTGAGE LIFE INSURANCE

This is a policy that provides funds to pay off a mortgage if the principal wage earner dies during the term of that loan. If you're at all concerned about this, look into purchasing term life insurance instead. With mortgage life insurance you are paying the same premium even though the amount of coverage is decreasing from year to year. Term life insurance becomes decreasingly expensive, since the coverage goes down as the mortgage decreases.

If you still have questions about insurance, contact your state insurance department. You might also call the Insurance Information Institute, the educational arm of the industry, at its toll-free hotline 1-800-221-4954. They provide brochures and fliers on insurance for the public.

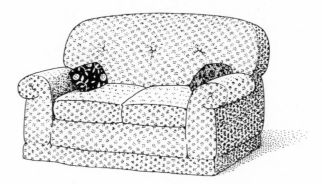

Condos and Co-ops

If you live in a condominium or cooperative, you will need two policies: one is purchased by the owners' association or co-operative board for the entire complex, for which you pay a pro-rated share of premiums as part of your monthly maintenance fee; the second is bought as coverage for your own unit and its possessions—a special policy for condominium owners, rent-ers' insurance for co-op dwellers.

The Importance of Taking Inventory

It's a nuisance and it's boring, but think about the importance of taking an inventory of your possessions. If your word pro-cessor or your Great Aunt Rose's brooch is stolen, how will you identify it if it is recovered? A description of the brooch is pos-sible, but how do you describe a word processor so the police know it's yours?

Here's another scenario. You return from work to find your place ransacked. After calming down a little, you try to tell the police what was stolen. But can you remember everything? Are there items you will not even know are missing? Do you really have a mental inventory of all your husband's possessions? Does he know every item in your jewelry box?

So you need an inventory—for the police, for the IRS, and for insurance purposes.

This does not mean counting every sheet and pillowcase, but rather making note—on paper—of the items of value you own. You can purchase inventory forms at a stationery store or you can call the Insurance Information Institute for a free copy of one.

In the main, you are going to note items of value in each room, the date of purchase, price (receipt attached to the inventory form, if possible), present value, and serial numbers, if available.

Even better is filling out your written inventory with pictures of every wall of each room, with cabinet and storage doors open. On the back of each photo, write the date and identify the room.

Store your inventory someplace outside your home for safekeeping, with a copy kept where you live. Update it from time to time, too.

Many police departments around the country offer a free service whereby you can borrow an etching tool to put an identification of some sort on items that carry none, such as bicycles, typewriters, and other household valuables. If yours does, you can borrow that etcher for the weekend and guarantee that in the event of theft your possessions are readily identifiable.

KEEPING IN TOUCH WITH YOUR POLICY

You cannot forget about insurance once you have taken out a homeowner's policy. You will need to check your coverage annually and update it if housing prices rise and the replacement cost of your home goes up, if you've made substantial improvements or built an addition, or if you've purchased new furnishings. An "inflation guard" policy that automatically adjusts your coverage each year to cover rises in building costs covers only inflation, so you cannot rely on that for total security.

Homeowner's insurance is a subject frequently given short shrift, but consider what you have to lose here: your home and, in a true disaster, all the furnishings in it. Don't make the mistake of becoming "insurance poor," signing up for every available policy because you are nervous or think you should have that particular coverage. But, after listening to your agent or broker, do purchase adequate protection for your castle.

15

HOW TO APPLY FOR—AND SECURE—A MORTGAGE

I f you think planning a wedding is nerve-racking, you will notice familiar twitches and nail biting when you begin to think about a mortgage. This is serious business, and while the panic does fade in buying one's second, third, and subsequent homes, there is always a *little* apprehension when you approach a lending institution for a home loan. You hold your breath: Will we be accepted? Will there be any snags? What if . . . ?

It is a *very* difficult time.

The one way to make things a little smoother is to educate yourself about the process so that you are in control and know what is coming next. You do not want to be assaulted by a strange battery of programs known only by initials.

What follows is an explanation of how the mortgage application—and approval—process works, from the beginning. By walking through the process, figuratively speaking, at your leisure, you can prepare yourselves, and your financial statements, for meetings with lenders. (Note: In a few parts of the country "trust deeds" take the place of mortgages. Here, a third-party trustee, not the lender, holds title to the property until the loan is paid. For ease in reading, however, the term "mortgage" will be used in this chapter.)

Starting Early

Ideally, thinking about a mortgage should begin before house-hunting, although most househunters look for both a home and a loan at about the same time. Contact at least three, preferably six, mortgage lenders in your area. Ask what their criteria for lending are, so you can get an idea of just what will be expected of you. Requirements vary from one lender to another, but there are similarities, too. Many will offer pre-approved loans, whereby the lender, after okaying your application, gives you a line of credit up to a certain amount. Some lenders do not prequalify, however, and you cannot make a formal application for a mortgage with them until you have the address of the property you wish to buy. You can, of course, ask questions about the market in general, and about your own financial situation.

It *is* important to shop around. Since lenders' terms are not all the same, the loan you secure from one institution can save you—or cost you—several thousand dollars over what is being offered by the one on the other side of town. Keep a listing of just what you learn from each institution, so that you can compare requirements and benefits (see the "Copy This . . ." box, page 217).

You can expect friendly, courteous treatment from mortgage loan officers, unless economic times are very tight and they are not interested in making loans. After all, the business of these institutions is lending money. In a slack market, they will be *delighted* to talk to you. Keep that in mind if the jitters set in with each call.

WHO LENDS?

First-time buyers frequently say "the bank" when talking about securing mortgage money, but in fact, there are several sources of those loans. Mutual savings banks and savings and loan associations are a principal source of mortgage money. Commercial banks lend money, too. Finance companies, affiliated or

THREE MARRIAGES, THREE MORTGAGES

Paula and Ed are both teachers in their early thirties. They expect increases in their salaries over the years, but unless they make a major career switch, they more or less know what their incomes will be in the school system where they are now employed. Those salaries are not grand—a joint $41,000. They like their work, however, and plan no change.

The house they chose was an older home in an established neighborhood, which they purchased for $107,000. The down payment was $17,000, put together from savings and some money awarded Paula from a divorce settlement several years back. After much number crunching, the couple decided a *thirty-year, fixed-rate mortgage* would be best for them. A loan of $90,000 at 10½ percent would mean monthly payments of $808. That, they felt, was comfortable. They were eager to start a family and wanted no surprises from rising interest rates. They also did not want to be forced to pay off a loan in just fifteen or twenty years, considering the higher monthly payments that would bring.

Toni and Roger elected to buy a condominium. They were able to put $20,000 on the $120,000 home they chose, money that came from savings. Their mortgage then was $100,000. However, this couple do not plan to stay in that home, or that town, more than two or three years. They both are young advertising agency employees in Chicago (with a joint income of $55,000),

---

wholly owned by large real estate agencies or franchises, also make these loans. If your husband is a veteran, or if you are the widow of a veteran, you can look into a mortgage from the Veterans Administration (VA), which makes direct loans to those individuals. Similarly, the Farmers Home Administration (FmHA) has several direct loan programs available for purchase of property in rural (note: *not* suburban) areas.

Next we come to mortgage bankers. These are companies that qualify applicants, find the best available loans for them, and then sell that loan to another lender or investor. That other investor may be, for example, a large pension fund, or a huge life insurance company that holds a portfolio of mortgages. You continue paying the mortgage banker after the sale of your loan.

and hope to move to Manhattan eventually. They had no need of the assurance offered by a locked-in interest rate for thirty years, so they opted for the fluctuating adjustable rate mortgage (ARM). The low first-year introductory rate might bring a rise of, at the most, two points a year, six points over the life of the loan. But the couple plan to have sold their condo by the end of two, or certainly three years. Their *thirty-year ARM at 7¾ percent for the first year* calls for a monthly payment of $707. Important: in thinking short-term, remember that a charge of one or more points can cancel out the advantage of the lower ARM rate. Toni and Roger paid no points.

Ellie and Phil went condo shopping, too. Young and with only a few years of work experience, they needed a low-cost home and attractive financing that included a minimal down payment. Their choice was a $65,000 condo, financed with *an FHA-insured loan*. The down payment was $3,250, the interest rate on their thirty-year loan 10½ percent. The monthly mortgage payment came to $550. Ellie manages a card shop; Phil owns and operates a small printing business. Their combined income is $30,000. Both needed and wanted the stability of a fixed interest rate, and feel they may well be in that condo for three, four, or more years. They cannot afford the shock of rises in an adjustable rate loan. They know, too, that when they do plan to move, the fact that FHA-backed mortgages are assumable will make their condo more attractive to buyers if interest rates have increased since their purchase.

Then there are mortgage *brokers*. (Getting confused?) These folks will find you a lender, for a fee. They do not lend the money themselves, but you must pay them all the application and processing fees you would pay a lender. When a lender is found, you pay those fees again to that institution. Mortgage brokers can be of most use in times of very tight money or when you are so pressed for time their services become worth the fee. Their fees vary widely, from 1 to 3 percent of the loan, sometimes more.

The seller of a house can also offer you a mortgage, but for the most part this is likely to happen only in a poor market for sellers. In good times, those parties do not need to offer assistance to buyers.

CONTACTING LENDERS

There are a number of questions you will want to ask of each institution. You many want to have them written down and in front of you so that you do not forget the especially important ones.

- *"What types of financing do you have available?"* Does the institution offer both fixed-rate and adjustable loans? (More about those mortgage choices later.) What about VA-insured loans and those from the Federal Housing Administration (FHA)? The latter are very popular with first-time buyers because they carry low down-payment requirements. There are ceilings to mortgages the FHA will grant, but they are not low. Some lenders and real estate agents do not advertise the availability of these programs because of the paperwork involved. Look into this type of financing, though, if it suits your purposes. It is worth the effort.

- *"What are the current rates for the loans you offer?"* This is very important since, as mentioned above, rates can differ considerably from one lender to another *and even from one program to another within one institution.*

- *"What is the term on these types of loans? Are they thirty-year fixed-rate loans? Adjustable rates running fifteen years? Is there a lower rate of interest for the shorter-term loans?"*

- *"What is your minimum down payment requirement?"* If you think you might not have all of the down payment, you can follow with *"Is private mortgage insurance being used here?"* This is an insurance policy that allows first-time buyers to purchase homes with a 5 percent down payment. There's more about this in Chapter 13.

- *"How do you qualify buyers?"* The loan officer will tell you if the institution grants mortgages for no more than two times the borrower's gross income or if you will be allowed to take on more debt.

- *"If we have a checking or savings account, or certificates of deposit here, are we entitled to preferred customer benefits?"* You may qualify for a slightly lower interest rate if you are a steady customer.

- *"How long will it take to get a mortgage commitment from you?"* You need to know this if you will have to give notice thirty days prior to leaving your apartment. Some commitments take only a week or two, but in a busy market, you may be waiting four, five or more weeks.

- *"How long will that mortgage commitment at the quoted rate be guaranteed?"* Usually a lender offers a ninety-day commitment, with renewals available. For new construction, you may have even more time. This becomes important if the closing date on your house is rescheduled many times, and if interest rates are steadily rising and you want to stay locked in to the lower rate on that commitment.

- *"What is your mortgage application fee?"* This usually runs from $100 to $300, and is nonrefundable.

A Variety of Programs

It is impossible to say which mortgage is best for you without knowing your personal situation and the state of the housing market in your area at the time you are buying. This is a decision you will have to make yourselves. Nonetheless, the "Three Marriages, Three Mortgages" box, page 202, offers an analysis of how some couples chose the financing right for them. One of those situations may parallel yours.

Here is what most lenders will offer, in one form or another, and what that loan will entail.

THIRTY-YEAR FIXED RATE

An old standby, this remains the best bet for most homeowners. The mortgage is paid off in thirty years.

Advantages: The monthly principal and interest payment are lower than they would be on a shorter-term loan, which can be financially more comfortable for some homeowners. You do not have to worry about your payments going up, and you can pay off the loan before the thirty years are up, if there are no penalties for prepayment, by making extra monthly principal payments when you can.

Disadvantages: You will be paying much more in total interest over the life of the mortgage than you would with a shorter-term loan. If you take out this loan originally at, say, an 11 percent interest rate, and four years later rates are more commonly 8½ percent, you will want to refinance the loan, which will cost you the equivalent of a new set of closing costs.

FIFTEEN-YEAR FIXED RATE

This loan is, of course, paid off in half the time of the thirty-year mortgage.

Advantages: Here you pay much less interest by paying off the loan more quickly. You build up equity more quickly, too.

Disadvantages: Your payments will be about 20 percent higher than they would on a thirty-year, fixed-rate loan.

ADJUSTABLE RATE MORTGAGE (ARM)

Interest rates are adjusted periodically, according to some pre-determined index—every year for one-year ARMs, every three years for three-year ARMs.

Advantages: The opening rate on an ARM is lower—sometimes significantly lower—than on a long-term fixed-rate mortgage. You may be able to afford a larger mortgage than you could if the loan had locked-in terms.

Disadvantages: Unfortunately, that terrific low introductory interest rate is likely to rise in the second year. It will go up in subsequent years, too, if market rates increase. Most rate increases are capped, however, at two percentage points annually, to a maximum five or six points over the life of the loan. *Be sure you secure an ARM with caps.* Try for a one-point rise in a year, four points over the life of the loan. This is a little more difficult to secure than the two–six increase, but it's worth it.

CONVERTIBLE ARM

This is an ARM that can be converted to a fixed-rate loan. The length of that fixed rate remains the same as your ARM—fifteen years, say.

Advantages: Usually you stand to get good terms here—the lower interest rate of an ARM, with the ability to be locked into a fixed interest if you see rates start to shoot up.

Disadvantages: You may find that lenders charge higher origination fees, higher rates, or steep conversion fees when they make convertible ARMs. The typical conversion fee (from ARM to fixed-rate) is about $250 to $300. Also, not all lenders offer the convertibles.

A special note about ARMs: These mortgages rise or fall with a particular index selected by each lending institution. Lenders make their selections based on an analysis of how they can best protect their loan portfolios. About half peg their ARMs to the one-year Treasury bill rate, which can be volatile but also attractive when interest rates fall. Ask about any other index your lender might use. Some, like the national Federal Home Loan Bank cost-of-funds, are broader-based indices that change more slowly.

THE BIWEEKLY MORTGAGE

This carries a regular fixed rate of interest, but instead of making a mortgage payment every month, you pay half a monthly payment every two weeks.

Advantages: You pay off your loan sooner, and you pay much less in total interest than you would with twelve monthly payments. A homeowner with a $100,000, thirty-year mortgage at 10 percent interest would save $77,635 in interest over the life of a loan by signing up for this program.

Disadvantages: With most shorter-term loans you get an accompanying lower rate of interest. You don't get that lower rate here. Also, can you afford what amounts to an additional monthly payment each year (it works out to be the equivalent of thirteen monthly payments instead of the twelve found in the more common once-a-month programs)?

ADJUSTABLE FIXED RATE

This is a loan that can be reset one time during the life of the mortgage, at the homeowner's request.

Advantages: You don't have to worry about being locked into a long-term fixed rate.

Disadvantages: There can be a lot of restrictions. You will probably be allowed to switch rates only between the start of the second year and the end of the fifth year of the loan. Maybe interest rates will have to drop a full two points in your area before an adjustment can be made. It is likely you'll have to pay a switching fee of $200 to $300.

SOME OTHER MORTGAGE CONSIDERATIONS

Your mortgage lender may also tell you you will be charged "points" for your loan. A point is equal to 1 percent of a loan. If you want a $120,000 mortgage, a point will be $1,200. Lenders can charge as many points as they like, depending on the economy at the moment, their general policy, where your house is located, or your financial profile. *You* may have to pay three points, the next applicant five. Points are payable at the closing (see more about closing costs in Chapter 16). When you are offered a choice of paying, let's say, two points or taking a mortgage with an interest rate a fraction of a percentage point lower, get out your calculator. Points are a nuisance to all mortgage shoppers, but they may well be cheaper than the higher interest rate you will be carrying with you for the long life of a loan.

Charges for paying your mortgage late is obviously not a subject you would want to bring up with a mortgage loan officer, but you should know that most lenders do penalize borrowers for missing a monthly payment deadline. Often there is a free grace period of a week or two, but then late charges are levied, and they can run from 2 percent to 10 percent of the unpaid amount.

"Assumption" is a term you may hear while talking to lenders. This means the interest rate on your loan can be taken on by the buyer of your house when you sell, a very attractive deal indeed if that rate is low. If your mortgage contract says that that debt can be assumed by the next buyer, it may prove an attractive sales tool for you. Most fixed-rate mortgages are not assumable these days, but FHA- and VA-backed loans are, and ARMs usually are. Still, if your lender retains the right to raise the interest rate, having the right of assumption loses some of its value.

WOULD YOU BELIEVE . . . ?

You know that you pay a good deal in interest over the life of a mortgage. If you do not want to know exactly how much the home you are buying may cost you, read no further.

Still with us? If you have a $150,000 mortgage at 10 percent interest running for thirty years, you will have paid $473,883.14 in principal and interest by the end of that loan. Amazing, isn't it?

"Buydown" is an offer made by a seller, or a developer offering new homes for sale, to buyers in a slow market. Essentially, the seller or developer prepays, with the approval of the lender, a part of a buyer's interest rate for a specified period of time, generally two or three years. That allows the size of the buyer's monthly payments to be reduced during that period, which enables more buyers to qualify for mortgages. If no mention of a buydown is made in the buyer's market you find yourselves in, then bring up the subject with the seller or developer.

Also, in a very stagnant real estate market, when lenders are desperate to make loans, ask the loan officer for any *extras* the institution has to offer. You might be charged no points or perhaps receive a financial benefit in some other branch of the institution. Maybe you'll be given a Visa card, with the first year's fee waived and 1 or 2 percent knocked off your bill for a specified time. Many lenders advertise during rough times, offering all sorts of bonuses to loan applicants. Read these ads, of course, and weigh those lenders' terms along with others. If they're good, why *not* get a little something extra along with your mortgage?

While Househunting

A good purchase to make during these days is a small paperback that is sold in most large bookstores. Two such titles: *Mortgage Calculator Guide* and *Amortized Mortgage Payments.* Basically, it is just page after page of calculations. You can look up a mortgage figure, a rate of interest, the number of years you need to pay off that loan, and come up with your monthly mortgage payment. It's an invaluable help, far easier to use than paper and pencil, or even a calculator.

For example, let's say you see a home costing $105,000. Maybe, you figure, you can get the seller to accept $100,000. If you make a down payment of 15 percent, or $15,000, you'll need a mortgage of $85,000. By flipping through the book you'll see that an $85,000 mortgage at a rate of, say, 10½ percent for thirty years will cost you $763 a month. The same loan at fifteen years would mean monthly payments of $927.

When you find the home you want to buy, the real estate agent may refer you to the arm of his or her office for financing, or may have forms for you to fill out from a lender in town with whom that company does business. You can, of course, approach a different lender, whom you have chosen after shopping around.

What the Mortgage Lender Wants to Know About You

Whether you can afford that house, of course, but a good deal more, too.

Here is what lenders will consider in looking over your application and deciding whether to grant you a mortgage:

- *Your Income* Lenders will take into account only the income in your household now, not what it will be in six months when you finish training to be a paralegal. If you are seriously concerned about qualifying for a loan, it would be wise to wait that short half year until you are employed and your income can be listed as well as his.

  Lenders used to ignore the second income in a family— usually, obviously, the wife's. But times have changed, and two-career families are common, make more money than a family with only one source of income, and have fewer mortgage delinquencies. Mortgage lenders welcome them.

  An interesting point, if you are transferring and buying a home in your new locale: In the past, lenders rarely took into account the spouse's second income on a mortgage application because that individual was usually temporarily without a job. Now things have changed a little, and a growing number of institutions are changing their policies for couples who are relocating. They have started counting up to 75 percent of the jobless spouse's previous income when examining an application from a transferred couple. This is done very carefully, however. Your career may be evaluated, with lenders considering some professions, like nursing and engineering, preferable since they are frequently in demand. If you are a free-lance graphic artist, for instance, that may be another story, although not necessarily a hopeless one.

Other lenders require that couples put in escrow an amount covering six months of mortgage payments, to be returned when the jobless spouse has found work.

How large a mortgage can you afford? Again, requirements vary and no numbers are carved in stone. There are guidelines, however.

Some lenders use the *income-to-housing-costs formula* to determine how much mortgage they will grant. Anticipated housing expenses are computed. These include mortgage payment, real estate taxes, and any house-related insurance. The total monthly figure for those costs must not exceed 25 to 28 percent of the gross household income of the applicant. Some lenders, however, are approving loans when and where housing costs are higher.

Then there is the *income-to-long-term-debt-payment formula.* Instead of using just housing costs, all of the borrower's long-term debts are calculated. These include car payments, child-support and alimony payments, outstanding credit-card and department store charge-card balances, education loans, and the like. You can qualify for a loan from most lenders who use this formula if the total monthly payments for housing expenses *and* long-term debts do not exceed 33 to 36 percent of the gross monthly income.

Bear in mind when doing your number crunching, however, that only *you* can determine how much mortgage you can comfortably carry. Lenders will not know how you plan to spend future income (indeed, an emergency may throw all your planning out of kilter). Are you adequately insured in the event of illness? Are your jobs reasonably secure? Are you planning a baby, with its attendant costs, in the near future? All of this should be weighed when considering whether to pursue the most expensive house for which you can qualify, or one you can pay for with relative ease.

- *Assets*   Another point that will interest lenders is your assets. Do you have a savings account? Bank certificates? Stocks or bonds? A car or two? Some vacant land? Do you have a trust account that will be handed over to you at a certain age? All assets should be listed, since the lender will be interested in knowing you do have the backup, if it is needed, of *something* of value.

- *Your Debts*   These are important, too. You will have to list car payments, credit-card and other "plastic" charges, education loans and any other sources of debt. Don't skip anything. Lenders will check with a credit reporting agency to obtain your credit record, and if they discover an enormous department store balance you "forgot" to mention, it won't do your application any good.

- *Your Credit Report*   The mortgage lender will contact one of the area credit-reporting agencies for a file on your debt payments. Note: This is not a credit "rating." The agencies supply only facts, not opinions about your creditworthiness. If you think there may be some problem in this area, check your Yellow Pages under Credit Reporting Agencies and find the company that has you in its file. For a fee of about $10, they will send you a copy of that file. You may want to see in advance what a lender will be checking, in order to make any changes, or perhaps add an explanation to what is on file. For example, if two years ago, when you were very ill and out of work for a while, you fell seriously behind in paying some bills for a few months, you would want to add that explanation to the report.

HOW WILL YOU LOOK TO A MORTGAGE LENDER?

GOOD	NOT SO GOOD
• Reasonably long employment at one place, with regular advancement and salary increases.	• Too many job changes without advancement or salary increases
• Working for a respectable, even well-known firm	• Doing too much moonlighting. (Being self-employed also makes things tough, but not impossible. You'll have to submit tax returns for the last two years. You may have to shop around, too. One way around all this is a down payment of 25 to 35 percent and an excellent credit report. It makes you eligible for a low documentation loan.)
• Good credit report	• Poor credit report or none at all. Paying cash is not virtuous when you need to build a solid credit history. To start one, take out a small bank loan and repay it promptly. Or make a major purchase at a department store, using their line of credit.
• Savings account, bank certificates, etc., especially if they are at the institution to which you are applying for a mortgage	• No savings
• Over twenty-five years of age	• Under twenty-five years of age
• Buying a home in a good neighborhood	• Choosing a house in need of major repairs and/or in a neighborhood on the decline
• Large down payment	• Minimal down payment (this can be all right with some lenders if you have sterling credit and/or work credentials)

- *The Down Payment* A lender will want to know if you have that money, an amount to be determined by that institution. The figure used to be 10 percent but over the last several years it has risen steadily, until now it is more commonly 15 or 20 percent. The reason for lenders' caution? In the last few years, they've been burned by homeowners who defaulted on their mortgages and had little invested in their homes, thanks to low down payments. They could therefore walk away from their homes when financial times got rough. The houses reverted to the lenders, who usually wanted mortgage payments, not a house on their hands. (There is more about the down payment, and how you can put one together, in Chapter 13.)

- *The Address of the Property You Are Buying* The lender is interested in the stability of the neighborhood you have chosen, and the house itself should not be overpriced or require too many repairs. Lenders do not want to invest in homes they may have to reclaim through foreclosure one day and then be unable to sell themselves. To be very sure this property is a good investment, an appraiser from the lending institution goes through the house before the mortgage application is approved.

FOR FOUR-STAR APPLICANTS

Most lenders now offer what are known as "low doc" loans (short for "low documentation"). This program offers nearly instant approval—four days or less—to applicants with a spotless credit record and a down payment of at least 25 percent.

All this weighing—of you and your income and assets, your down payment, the property itself and its value in today's real estate market—will be taking place during the weeks you are waiting for your mortgage to be approved. Remember, while you are becoming increasingly nervous, the overwhelming number of mortgage applications *are* okayed (banks are in the business to lend money, remember?). You're likely to be one of the lucky ones. One fine day your real estate agent will call, or perhaps the call will come from the lender. He or she will not sound excited. This is just routine business for them, after all. Quite matter-of-factly you will be told your mortgage has been approved and the closing for your house has been set for such-and-such a date.

Next, a written mortgage commitment will be sent to you, or to your real estate agent or attorney. Whew! Now it's time for the first easy breath you've taken in weeks.

COPY THIS . . .

. . . and use it to compare lending terms at the institutions you contact.

Lender _____

Address _____

Phone _____ Contact _____

Mortgage application fee _____

Mortgage programs offered _____

_____

_____

_____

_____

Limit on loan amount _____

Loan qualification guidelines _____

_____

_____

_____

_____

Down-payment requirement _____

Points charged _____

Benefits for customers _____

Length of loan commitment (is it renewable?) _____

Rate guarantee commitment? _____

Comments and notes _____

_____

_____

_____

_____

Note: You may also want to ask about charges that will be included in closing costs, such as the loan origination fee (not to be confused with mortgage application fee); appraisal fee; and the like (more about them in Chapter 16). It is not likely, however, that you will choose a mortgage lender on the basis of those charges.

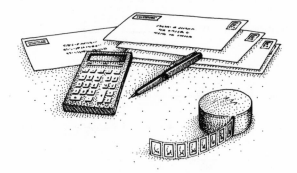

AS YOU MOVE CLOSER TO BUYING . . .

	YES	NO
Do you *both* talk enthusiastically about this buying decision, rather than one of you appearing to be more eager than the other?		
Are you able to talk over homebuying jitters either of you may be feeling, whether serious or seemingly foolish?		
Do you agree how the mortgage shopping (phone calls, visits to lenders) will be conducted? Will you do it? Will he? Will you spend lunch hours visiting banks together?		
You could buy the most expensive house you can carry on your incomes, or one kinder to your budget. Is the choice you made comfortable for both of you?		
If you are both employed, have you looked ahead to meeting a monthly mortgage payment if you should retire to have a baby and perhaps stay home several months or a few years?		

	YES	NO
Are you psychologically prepared, if need be, to see most or all of your savings disappear into a down payment on a house?		
Are you both committed to building up that reserve again?		
If you have already chosen the house you want to buy, do you both like it equally, give or take a few minor features?		

Last question: Are most of your answers in the "Yes" column? Good. You may both want to talk a little more about those few "No" responses.

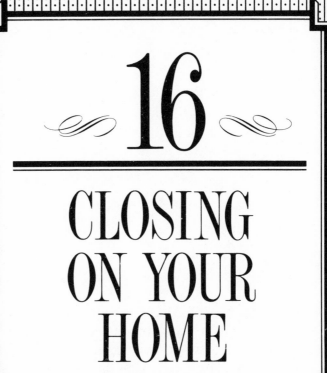

16

CLOSING ON YOUR HOME

After you receive a mortgage commitment from the institution that will grant you that loan, the lender will set a date for the closing (or "settlement," as it is also called). This may be four weeks or longer, from the date of the commitment.

The closing occurs when the property actually changes hands from seller to buyer. It is a meeting attended by the sellers, the buyers, and their attorneys, if they have them; the real estate agent; and a representative from the lending institution. This can make for quite a crowded room (the scene may be the lender's office, or the office of one of the attorneys, or some other location).

In some areas of the country—California, for one—the closing is handled by an escrow company, rather than separate attorneys, and neither buyer nor seller has to be present for a closing.

How You Will Own Your Home

There are three basic ways in which title can be held by home-buyers, only one of which concerns you: (1) Tenants by entirety for husband and wife. Under this arrangement, both of you own the property jointly, with what is known as a "right of survivorship." If one party dies, the other automatically owns the entire property, without having to go through probate court for distribution of that asset. For your own information, the other styles of ownership are (2) joint tenants with right of survivorship, which is similar to the above, only the parties are not married; and (3) tenants in common, where each buyer has a divisible interest in the property to the extent of his or her ownership. It can be split equally, or one party can own a larger share than the other. With tenants in common, each can will his or her share of the property to anyone at all. It does not revert to the other owner.

Taking Possession Before Closing

You are so eager to move into your new home that you think you just might do that before the closing. Or perhaps you have no place else to go, and so are thinking of taking possession of the house before the settlement date.

Ask your attorney before you take that step. If he or she concurs, and the sellers will have vacated the home and are amenable to your moving in, you will probably pay them rent for the days you live there before taking title. This should not be undertaken without counsel, however.

A Laundry List of Charges

Let's get back to that auspicious day, the closing. What, exactly, are you expected to pay for at this point?

Somewhere between the commitment letter and the settlement date, your lending institution will send you a U.S. government pamphlet explaining closing costs. These are often expenses a brand-new homeowner has not considered, but you, of course, have read about them in earlier chapters here.

The fees can vary from one lending institution to another, but in general they cover the following:

- *Loan Origination Fee*   This covers processing costs.

- *Appraisal Fee*   This is the charge the lender makes for having the house you want to buy appraised.

- *Credit Report Fee*   Sometimes this is charged when you make an application for a mortgage, sometimes at settlement.

- *Title Insurance*   This protects the lender against claims to ownership of your home by anyone but you while they hold the mortgage.

- *Recording and Transfer Fee*   This covers legally recording the new deed and mortgage (you receive copies too). City, county and/or state stamps may also be required, and they also carry a fee.

- *Settlement Agent's Fees*   These can be charged by the lender's attorney or an escrow company.

- *Points*   A "point" equals 1 percent of a loan. Lenders can charge points if they choose, the most common number being between one and three. Points are payable up front at the closing. This is a charge you are prepared for, of course, since you learned when you applied for the mortgage how many points the lender required.

- *Interest*   Buyers must usually pay interest on their loan for the period between the closing date and the date that the first scheduled loan payment is due.

- *Private Mortgage Insurance*   If this is required of you, some part of the premium will be due in advance and you must show proof to the lender that you have made one month's payment or one-quarter of the annual premium. Sometimes the full first year's premium is payable by the closing.

- *Homeowner's Insurance*   You will have to show proof that you have this policy (see Chapter 14 for more about homeowner's insurance). Bring a letter from the insurance company attesting to the existence of your policy or, better yet, a canceled check for the first payment you have made (or whatever percentage of the first year's bill the lender requires).

- *Flood or Other Hazard Insurance*   This insurance may be required where you live, and you may need proof of coverage.

- *Taxes*   Most lenders require a regular monthly payment to a reserve account for city and/or county property taxes. You will probably pay a certain amount each month for taxes, along with your mortgage payment. When taxes are due in your municipality—usually quarterly—the lender makes those payments for you. Lenders also require an amount equal to six months' taxes to be paid at the closing and held in an escrow account (try to get interest on this escrow money).

There may be other fees you will be responsible for at the closing ceremony, charges peculiar to your own area of the country or to your lending institution. The ones mentioned above, however, are the most common.

The Real Estate Settlement and Procedures Act of 1974 mandated full disclosure of fees charged in the transfer of property, so that buyers no longer need to go to a closing not knowing how much money they are going to have to fork over and—almost worse—worrying about whether they have enough.

Besides sending you the government booklet outlining settlement procedures, the lending institution will send you a form with items listed and the specific amount you will be required to pay for each item. Check with your attorney a few days before closing and have him verify closing costs with the lender, so that you will find no unwelcome surprises on closing day. If you want to feel super-secure, bring extra money with you. In some states, attorneys do most, if not all, of the paperwork needed for the closing. At the very least, they review all documents involved in that transaction to protect their clients' interests.

If you still have questions about any aspect of the settlement, call the lender, your attorney, or the real estate agent for answers.

In addition to the charges mentioned above, you will have to pay your attorney's fee, usually at the closing, but he or she may bill you after that date. If the house has oil heat, you may have to hand the seller a check for the estimated amount of any oil left in the tank. You do *not* have to pay a real estate agent's commission; that is picked up by the seller of the house. Mortgage brokers' fees are paid here, too.

What, exactly, is all this going to cost you? Around 3 to 5 percent of the cost of your mortgage. If you are taking out a loan of $120,000, for example, closing fees can range from $3,600 to around $6,000. And this *must* be paid in full on the day of settlement. Check with your attorney about the advantages of cashier's checks over personal checks, or vice versa, for payment.

Some points to keep in mind:

- Closing dates are not carved in stone. They can be changed a few times to fit the schedules of the parties involved. This can drive buyers totally crazy (or the sellers, since they can be inconvenienced too), especially if the new owners are planning to give up an apartment on June 30 following a June 28 closing and now learn over the phone that the lender has set a new closing date of July 15. Try to anticipate the possibility of date changes when making your own moving plans.

- Prior to the settlement, you are allowed to "walk through" the home you have purchased to see that no disaster (the roof has leaked all over the bedroom ceiling) has befallen it since you "bought" it two months earlier. This should be done a few days before the closing, giving the owner time to correct any problems, show that work to make repairs is in progress, or offer cash so that *you* can make the repairs.

- You may have a pleasant relationship, if there is any at all, with the sellers of the home, but many buyers do not. Do not be surprised, therefore, if negotiations over price, the house inspection, or some other aspect of the sale has produced a coolness between you and seller. Be grateful it hasn't escalated into war. One couple recalled that, at their closing, the seller threw the keys to the house at them across the table!

It will, finally, be over. You or your husband will pocket the house keys. There are apt to be smiles all around (the sellers, though, may still be cranky), and your real estate agent may take you to lunch. It is a day for celebration, a milestone in your lives. Enjoy it to its very last moment!

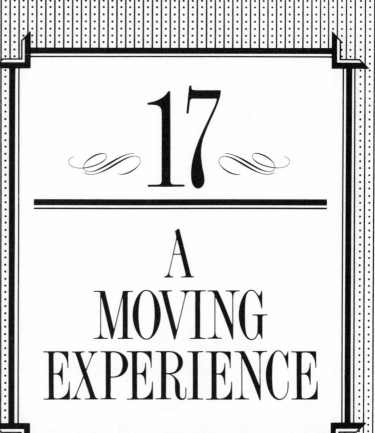

17

A
MOVING
EXPERIENCE

You're probably pleased to be moving. Perhaps you are trading up—to a larger apartment, a more desirable location, your first home. But no matter how happy you are at the thought of being in the new place, the idea of *getting* there makes for major anxiety. No one enjoys the process of moving, although 20 percent of all Americans do pick up stakes and head for a new home every year.

Organization can make it all a lot smoother. The logistics of the basic bread-and-butter move can be broken down into five stages:

Step 1:
Know Where You're Heading

Not as obvious as it sounds. Yes, you're moving from Sweetstown to Pleasantville, but do you know what awaits you there besides your new home? One of the anxieties of moving is the unknown that a new community brings. To alleviate this stress, try to familiarize yourself with Pleasantville while you're still at your current address. If your new home is several towns over, a county away, the other end of the state or even farther, try to get a short-term subscription to the local newspaper there. From the news articles, you'll learn what concerns the residents now—zoning issues, any environmental problems, political structure, social chitchat. Maybe there are clubs you'll recognize and are prepared to join, or charity work that attracts you. From a business standpoint, the paper offers all sorts of opportunities. If you're self-employed, offering a product or service, learning who your customers are likely to be is invaluable. If you will be job hunting, reading about openings gives you a head start.

Adrienne and Dwayne moved when he was offered a job by one of the major-league baseball farms. Adrienne was a legal secretary; she read the paper from the southern town to which they were moving to get a sense of where the jobs were and what they paid. "I was happy for Dwayne," she recalls, "but a little concerned for me. I wanted to start working reasonably soon after the move, so I sort of knew what was waiting for me when we got there by reading the paper first. There was also a city magazine I read, which didn't mention job offerings, but did give me a flavor of that whole area. Coming from Minnesota, the South was totally new to me."

Adrienne did secure a job two weeks after the move, from an employment agency whose ads she had seen often in the newspaper. She began working even before the couple had finished unpacking! "I took a cue from how Dwayne was looking at it," she says. "Baseball was baseball to him, no matter where he played. So I figured legal work was legal work, and I'd have the stability of a familiar job while I was trying to get used to a new home and a new part of the country." Newspaper *advertisements* can give you an idea of stores and services available in the new town. And you'll find, as Adrienne did, that city magazines are another help. There are dozens of them, some covering one particular urban area, others entire regions. Any large newsstand will carry a selection of them. Your public library can provide names and addresses of newspapers around the country.

You might also contact the local Chamber of Commerce for printed materials they can send. And drop a line to the state Department of Tourism, located in the state capital, for still more brochures and fliers. Those folks can help you locate scenic and historic attractions around your new home; you will, after all, want to take in the sights, too.

If you're leaving the state, and you or your husband would like to be in touch with professional colleagues in your new locale, you can join the appropriate statewide associations before you move, and receive a list of members, their latest newsletter, and the like. Similarly, if you need professional licenses (to practice law, to work for some service agencies, for hairdressing, teaching, and so forth), those groups can assist you to secure credentials. You might also contact the state Department of Labor for further information about licensing.

Step 2:
What Moves with You, What Stays Behind

Just look at all you've accumulated, and you've been in your present home only six months—or has it been six years? The next step in preparing for the Move is to decide what goes in the moving van and what, sadly, will not get to make that historic journey. Start weeding out early—be ruthless. You can get rid of stuff any number of ways: by donating it to charities, selling certain items through classified advertisements, holding a garage or lobby or gate sale, or by hauling it all to a flea market in town.

Holding an auction is an option if you have valuable art, china, or collectibles. The auctioneer does the work for you and is paid either a flat fee or a percentage of the day's receipts. The auctioneer will also appraise what you want to sell.

Storage may be important now, too. Maybe there are some things you want to keep, but don't want to take with you right away, which can be stored in your folks' basement or attic. Or perhaps you have it all in a self-storage unit and want to leave it there and pay for the space long-distance. Another option: move it to a warehouse closer to your new home.

Step 3:
Which Mover?

If you are on a very tight budget, you may decide to do it all yourselves, perhaps with the aid of a few friends (only *very* good buddies will sign up for this chore!). This can work well if you are moving a few blocks or just a few miles and do not have many possessions. Treat your pals to dinner that evening, of course, if you all have the strength to make it to the nearest watering hole.

A step up from doing it yourself is hiring the guy who announces his services on a neighborhood bulletin board and hires two men to help him. This can cost you $30 or so an hour. The mover may provide you with some packing materials, but that is not likely. He may come over to look at your things and offer an estimate, or he may charge a flat hourly rate without making that visit. This can work out nicely—and for a reasonable fee— if you check references and your local Department of Consumer Affairs to see if these folks provide satisfactory service. Obviously, a personal reference is always welcome, too.

Your third choice is the licensed professional moving company, perhaps one of the nationwide outfits. Again, call to see if any complaints have been lodged with your local consumer protection agencies. It's difficult even to estimate what such a move will cost, but generally you can expect to pay from $400 for reasonably short moves to several thousand dollars for long-distance hauls of full households.

You can call the carriers you are considering and have someone come over to make an estimate. You should ask them if they will do the packing for you—and how much that will cost—or if you must do it all yourselves. Do they supply cartons, and wardrobes for clothes? For how much? Ask to look over the company's insurance coverage at this time, too.

(A couple of points to consider: Buying boxes from the carrier can be costly. Maybe heavy boxes you collect from grocery stores—liquor-store boxes are especially good—will do just as well. If you are now living in an apartment, you may want to check with the building manager or superintendent before setting a specific time for the move. Some buildings restrict moving in or out to certain days of the week, or within certain hours.)

COPING WITH STRESS

Moving brings stress, even a welcome move. You may find you need outside help to see you through the first few difficult weeks or months. You can call your local social services or human services agency for the name of a relocation counselor or therapist if there is one in your new locale. No such luck? Why not form your own small group by advertising on bulletin boards in your new area? Perhaps your library or a community service agency will offer you space for meetings. You can invite guest speakers, who can talk about the psychological trauma of moving, such as leaving parents, and perhaps siblings, for the first time, or difficulty in making new friends and coping with an interrupted career if you are not the transferred spouse.

It's smart to get two or three estimates from movers. For short, intrastate (within the state) moves of under forty miles or so, the estimate is based on the time the move is likely to take. Charges for interstate (from one state to another) moves will be based on the weight of the goods and the distance the movers will travel. Ask your mover's agent for the free Interstate Commerce Commission booklet *When You Move: Your Rights and Responsibilities.*

Some companies offer a binding estimate, while others may finally charge more than the estimate. (Guaranteed prices are illegal in some states, where costs must be based on either hours worked or the weight of the shipment.) Too great a discrepancy among bids may mean poorer service from the company coming in with the lowest figures. Remember, you pretty much get what you pay for. If you have a choice, is the binding estimate better than the nonbinding? That is difficult to say. Sometimes the binding estimate is higher because it *is* binding. The nonbinding may be better if it is a lower estimate than others—without a diminution of service—and if you are sure you have told each agent that the same items are going, and have not added pieces as you've talked to different movers. Note: government regulations say nonbinding estimates can be increased as much as 10 percent when it comes time to pay.

Payment to the moving company can be made with cash, by money order, bank check, or traveler's checks. Personal checks are not accepted. Some companies accept credit-card payments, although the carrier will have to check your credit with the card company before approving it. A very few companies allow payments to be made over an extended period, with interest attached.

Movers expect to be tipped. Some suggest 10 to 15 percent of the cost of the move, divided among all the movers. Others say $25 to $35 *per mover* would be satisfactory. Yes, that is a lot of money, but while a few moving companies still claim that a gratuity is up to the satisfied customer, the majority urge customers to tip. Consider these suggested figures, the practice in your part of the country, your satisfaction with the job, and how intimidated you are with the tipping process, and then tip accordingly.

The contract, or bill of lading, is the legal document you will sign with the moving company. Read it carefully. It should list the mover's name(s), address, state license number, and telephone number, along with the declared value of the goods, where they are heading, the loading date and the delivery date.

The bill of lading is also a listing of what you are sending to the new location. That part of the document will read something like: "1 coffee table chipped in one corner; 1 wicker trunk; 14 cardboard cartons POCU [packed by owner, condition unknown]."

Speaking of lists, you should be keeping your own list of what has gone into cartons. Give each box a room designation and a number, and in a notebook put down that number with an explanation next to it of what that box contains. If a box says "Kitchen 14," for example, you will know where the movers should put it, and that inside you will find your tablecloths, place mats, and napkins.

Check your homeowner's insurance policy to see if and how you are covered for goods in transit. You will also be able to purchase liability coverage from the mover. Be sure to read all of that company's offerings before making a decision. Movers cannot be held accountable for items not listed on the bill of lading, of course.

If you have valuable art or antiques, call them to the attention of the mover to be sure they are adequately covered. Check your own homeowner's or renter's insurance policy, too. It, or riders to it, may mention coverage during a move.

Step 4:
Moving

Lois Benjamin is president of Shleppers, a New York City moving company, which she and her husband, Shlomo, founded a little over ten years ago. Shleppers has three offices, two warehouses, and twelve commercial vehicles. Benjamin has moved several times and, having three small children, knows what it is to . . . well, to shlep.

She notes that while moving tends to be a man's business, it is women who often handle a family's actual move. She says:

"A lot of people think it's great to put everything in one box. But nobody can move that box. They think with fewer boxes they will save money, but ultimately you need more men to lift them, or maybe they can't be lifted at all. I'd say the rule here is the heavier the item you're moving is, the smaller the box. Books go into small boxes. Linens, which are very light, can be packed in larger boxes."

Benjamin finds large plastic trash bags another no-no for packing, because the goods inside are sometimes damaged; they would be better protected in cardboard boxes. "People will wrap paintings or mirrors in material instead of buying good boxes," she adds. "There's such a great chance of damaging them that it's silly."

She also cautions against packing personal belongings like jewelry or stock certificates. "They should be kept on your person," she says. "If people don't do that, they panic when they can't find them. More than ninety-nine percent of the time they're found, but why put yourself through that? It's such an upsetting

AVOID SUMMER, IF YOU CAN

Nearly two-thirds of all residential moves take place between May 1 and October 1. Avoid those months if at all possible, for easier scheduling and better attention. If you must move during the summer, schedule your date with the movers as far in advance as you can and, a week or so before the move, call to confirm. If you are buying a home and planning your move to coincide with the closing date, go ahead and line up the movers, even though there is a chance the closing will be rescheduled. You can always change the moving date. At least the movers will have visited your place for the estimate, will have answered any of your questions or concerns, and will have you on their schedule.

thing to move anyway. Besides, if you keep with you the things that are important to you, that helps you feel like you've got part of your home with you."

Some other tips: Remember if you are cushioning breakables with paper that newspaper can rub off on those items—china, for instance—and may permanently stain them. Try to make sure you have three or four inches of crumpled paper on the bottom of those boxes. To avoid becoming totally engulfed by the process, pack one room at a time, even though there might be the temptation to pack the books in the bedroom while you're looking at them, and put away the china on the knickknack shelf in the living room as *that* catches your eye.

During the few days, or weeks, before the move, you can notify utility companies in your present town about canceling services and in the new town about installing them. Same with the telephone company. The post office has a change-of-address form to fill out, so that mail will be forwarded. They can also help with forms to change your address on magazine subscriptions. On your own, you may want to photostat a letter, or perhaps have a printer make up cards, announcing your move to send to friends, business associates, doctors, dentist, banks, and others who will want—or need—to know your new address.

When you're completing your packing, fill one last box with items you will need immediately in your new home, and take it with you in your car (see the "The Box [or Two] That Goes With You" box, page 240).

On *the* Day, it is best to stay with the movers all the way to your new home, if you can. Or, if that is not possible, have someone at the new location wait for them. If there is no one there to greet them, movers have the right to leave all your possessions right on your doorstep.

If you are being charged an hourly rate, note on the bill of lading both the starting and finishing times.

Do not sign the bill of lading—and be sure to tell this to the friend who may be waiting in New Town to greet the movers for you—until you have examined at least the most important or fragile of your possessions to be sure they survived the journey. On the contract you can note any damage and add something like "approved subject to unpacking boxes." These words may be all the proof you have if something goes wrong and you need to document your case.

What happens if something is badly damaged during the move and you are not satisfied with the company's settlement? With many movers, unresolved disputes go to binding arbitration. This means you must accept the decision of an arbitrator. If, after the arbitration, you still have complaints about a move within your area, you can contact your state Department of Transportation. Complaints about a move to another state should be directed to the Interstate Commerce Commission. You can write the ICC, Office of Compliance and Consumer Assistance, Room 6328, 12th and Constitution Ave. N.W., Washington, D.C. 20423, or telephone (202) 275-7844.

Can moving expenses be deducted from your federal tax return? *Only* if the move is made because you are starting work at a new location. Even in that event, the deduction comes with a list of restrictions. Check with your accountant.

Step 5:
Settling In

Presumably the new house or apartment will be clean, thanks to your predecessors, yourselves, or a cleaning service you hired in advance. No point in unpacking boxes or moving furniture around when the place needs a good scrubbing. Do the kitchen first, since there are many items that can't be stored until you put up spice racks, paper-towel holders, pot racks, and the like.

Lois Benjamin suggests a system she adapted for her most recent move: hiring the movers to *unpack*. "People don't use that service a lot because it's expensive," she explains. "But I thought it was great. I had three guys in the kitchen unpacking everything while I put it away. When they got too fast, they helped me. I had the kitchen unpacked in an evening, and they took away all the boxes and the wrapping paper."

Still, she adds: "You don't need that in every room—you'd want to do closets and personal things on your own.

"This may cost you another hundred dollars, but it saves you weeks of work. I should think for newlywed couples, especially, it would be valuable. They want to get settled in and start playing house."

The bathroom should be easy to organize, since it requires little more than a shower curtain and window blinds, shades or curtains, and perhaps some small racks for toiletries. Figuring out the living room may take longer as you discuss alternative furniture arrangements and wait for deliveries of new purchases. Don't despair if unpacking takes longer than you planned. If you both work and are tired at the end of the day, you may only have

THE BOX (OR TWO) THAT GOES WITH YOU

Here are the basics you will need to get along during the first day or so in your new home. You can pack them in a separate carton, to be taken with you in your car, but labeled clearly so that you can get to it immediately.

_____ tissues	_____ tool kit
_____ bed linens	_____ extension cords
_____ towels	_____ shelf liner
_____ work clothes/loungewear	_____ a lamp
_____ nightgown, p.j.'s	_____ light bulbs
_____ personal items (tooth- brush, razor, etc.)	_____ garbage can/bags

Items you'll need for your first meals:

_____ disposable plates, cups, utensils	_____ soap, sponges
_____ can opener	_____ pots and pans
_____ aluminum or plastic wrap	_____ paper towels

Do you have a pet? Don't forget a food bowl, a water bowl, some food for the first couple of meals, and a few favorite toys.

weekends on which to paint, arrange furniture, put up book-shelves, and so forth. Don't rush it. Actually, by taking things slowly, you may come up with new decorating themes and may find new uses for old objects. Your imagination will be at work while you unpack—take a break, sit on the floor and think!

Kelly found a way around the common problem of bare windows and the inevitable wait for a shopping trip to pick out window dressings, plus another delay before hemming curtains or buying appropriate rods. "I bought a dozen tension rods in the five-and-ten," she explains. "They expand and contract inside the window frame, and I hung up whatever materials I had, just so all the windows looked neat. I didn't bother with hemming, and at the top of the rods I just folded the material over a little and pinned it. Some of the fabric was white sheets, some was other bits and pieces I had around. I only made half curtains, although in some rooms the curtains went about two-thirds up the window.

"Those would-be curtains kept me from panicking about having nothing up at the windows and gave us a chance to think about what we wanted before investing in blinds or shades."

There are steps you can take—once you have the strength—to make yourself at home more quickly in your new locale. Working can help, as business associates often become friends. Join a Newcomer's Club, which are groups found in many suburbs with high transient traffic.

In an apartment building or complex, introduce yourselves to the building manager, superintendent, or staff at the rental office. Attend tenants' meetings, if they exist. If the complex comes with a pool and a social calendar, you have a good head start toward becoming comfortably settled in. Let the mailman know you're living there, too, and get acquainted with local shopkeepers.

It won't take long. Soon you'll be walking toward your new home on automatic pilot, nodding to familiar faces, as comfortable there as you were where you lived before. Home, sweet home.

A Job Transfer?

Moving because one of you is being relocated by your company involves all of the foregoing procedures, plus some additional stresses and concerns.

Since this is a book about one's home, we'll concentrate on that aspect of relocation, without mentioning the wisdom of such a move in terms of long-range career plans (yours or his). Fortunately, most corporations are only too happy to ease the path between Town A and Town B these days, which alleviates a good deal of the nervousness about company transfers.

A 1988 Merrill Lynch relocation survey showed that, of the 613 large industrial and nonindustrial firms surveyed, 97 percent had some form of formal relocation policy; most firms are finding that, as the economy changes, they must continually update these policies. Companies that help employees with the sale of their homes are far more common nowadays, for example, than even as late as the early 1970s.

You may decide, when job relocation looms, that you will be a long-distance commuting couple. No one knows how many commuter marriages there are in the USA, but estimates by those in the relocation and job-counseling fields are anywhere from 700,000 to several million couples.

Commuter marriages are still not the norm, however, so you and your husband will probably pick up stakes and move when the job transfer call comes to one of you. (Women represent an estimated 10 to 15 percent of job transfers these days.) How do you do this wisely, from a real estate angle?

- The real estate aspect of your move may not seem as important if you are both young and on the first or second of many steps up the career ladder. But still, give this some thought. It may affect your financial future more than you realize, since what you are spending on this move can cut seriously into your savings, while day-to-day living in the new locale can also cost you money you do not anticipate, or wish to spend. If you are moving from Mobile to Los Angeles, for example, work the numbers in terms of the cost of living in L.A., the cost of homes, the size of your savings and your new income.

Moving to a higher-cost area is a prime reason many would-be transferees turn down relocation. Couples heading from either coast to a town somewhere in between are likely to fare well. Those moving from the heartland *to* either coast are apt to be stunned by the high cost of living and housing. If the "trailing spouse" will be job hunting, note that salaries are likely to be higher on the coasts, but those wages can be quickly eaten up by what it costs to live there. Similarly, making the switch from a high-cost area to one where living expenses are reasonable may also mean minimum salary levels for the spouse who must now seek employment. All of this should be discussed, of course, by the two of you.

- Once you've decided relocation is worth the effort, look into what your company offers in the way of assistance and perks. Company benefits tend to vary, according to the state of the economy, whether the transferee is heading for a higher-priced locale, and intangibles such as the value of the employee and desirability of the new location. And, of course, that particular company's relocation policy. Ask for as much as you can think of. No move, even with corporate assistance, is going to cost you nothing, but you can shave expenses considerably by having the company foot much of the bill.

- Guaranteed by just about every company these days is a no-cost househunting trip for two to the new locale. Your moving costs will be paid, of course, and so will virtually all other expenses connected with the housing end of the relocation—attorney's fees, pest inspection, radon test, most of the closing costs. Many companies also offer transferees a "bridge loan," if their house hasn't been sold before they buy the new one.

- If you have a house to sell, you have a few choices: you can ask the company to take it off your hands and sell it for you, which they may well do; or you can hold on to the house or condominium and rent it, considering it an investment. This can work, although being a long-distance landlord isn't the wisest strategy. Is there someone in your current hometown who might serve as sort of a superintendent for you? Someone who can check on the place periodically, someone the tenants can call when things go wrong? Also, consider rent. Will what you can get cover your expenses so that you avoid a negative cash flow? If rents are around $600 a month where you are now, and you are paying $1,100 a month in mortgage and real estate taxes, you're going to be out of pocket. Selling makes more sense, unless you plan to return to that home one day. Maybe your assignment is of one or two years' duration. If you truly love that house and realize you are losing money by holding on to it, you may decide it is worth the loss to know it is waiting there for you.

  Your third choice is to leave the house empty, move and allow a real estate agent to handle the sale for you. Or the transferee might move ahead, while the spouse stays behind to sell the house. Or perhaps you will keep the house, and one of you will continue living there if you decide to be a commuting couple.

  Try not to panic and sell if the market is poor. In that situation, consider renting, or trying to get a decent price from the corporation offering the transfer. Perhaps you will sell at the price you can get, while they make up the difference between that figure and what you could have realized in better market conditions. Some companies will buy the house from you outright.

- Ask the company about any cost-of-living allowances and cash benefits they might offer if you are moving to a high-cost housing locale. Perhaps these will take the form of an outright bonus or a long-term subsidy. Mention mortgage interest rates, too, if they are high at the time of your move. Some corporations will absorb a percentage point or a fraction of a point on the home you will buy in the new town so that you are not paying unnecessarily high interest because of the move.

RELOCATION SPECIALISTS

Some companies refer transferees to their own in-house relocation staff; others send employees to outside companies they retain, many of which are associated with real estate agencies. In the main, a relocation specialist can be expected to talk to you and your husband about your needs in the new community—the kind of housing you seek, your budget, and so forth. Then he or she will put you in touch with local real estate agents. The relocation agent will spell out how your company can assist you with this transfer and will arrange the move, explaining such finer points as the tax picture and how the company can help you with financing a home in the new locale and selling the old one, if you need assistance. The corporation pays for all of this, of course, and indeed, once you or your husband accepts the transfer, they may turn you right over to a relocation outfit. If you decide to keep your house and rent it, an employee transfer company will often find a tenant, collect rent, make mortgage payments, and supervise repairs, usually at a fee charged to the employee (unless the company picks up this tab as a perk for the transferee).

If the company offers no relocation assistance, you might want to consider signing up with a firm on your own. The two largest in the nation—Homequity and Merrill Lynch Relocation Management—have been joined by thousands of similar companies around the country, some that are one-person shops operating in a small community. The larger companies usually work only for corporations and will not take individual accounts, but the smaller ones will. To find one on your own, you can contact the Employee Relocation Council in Washington, D.C., an umbrella group of corporations that move their employees, relocation companies, real estate brokers, and others interested in the field. Their telephone number is (202) 857-0857.

You might also check the Yellow Pages under Relocation Services. By all means call the consumer protection agency in your area to see if any complaints have been filed against the individual or company you are considering. Costs vary. You may be charged a flat fee or an hourly rate. Most relocation specialists spend ten to fourteen hours with a client.

The bottom line here, though, is to look to the company transferring you or your husband to provide as much assistance, and as many financial benefits, as possible. These days more and more of them are doing just that.

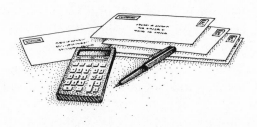

A MIXED BLESSING?

Are you both happy about the job transfer? Is one of you elated while the other is simply putting on a happy face? Or do you both wonder if relocating is the right move—literally—at this point in your lives? Here is a quiz to help you crystallize the pluses and minuses of the move. How do you feel about these aspects of what's ahead?

	VERY POSITIVE	SOMEWHAT CONCERNED	STRICTLY NEGATIVE	DOESN'T MATTER
For the transferred spouse:				
The new job				
For the trailing spouse:				
Finding work/continuing education in the new locale				
For both of you:				
Giving up the particular apartment/house we have — YOU / HIM				
Liking the city or town where we are heading — YOU / HIM				
Leaving family/friends — YOU / HIM				
Leaving behind civic/volunteer work I care about — YOU / HIM				

	VERY POSITIVE	SOMEWHAT CONCERNED	STRICTLY NEGATIVE	DOESN'T MATTER
Getting ready for the move (finding a new home, packing, etc.) — YOU				
HIM				
Settling into the new community — YOU				
HIM				
The sense that this move fits in with long-range career plans for both of us — YOU				
HIM				
Sustaining any financial loss in the move — YOU				
HIM				
Agreement on what we'll do if one of us does not like the new locale (after giving it a fair try) — YOU				
HIM				

18

AND NOW...
THE
HOUSEWARMING!

Y ou have bought or built your home. You have struggled through the complicated mortgage maze and have endured the stress of moving. Now you are in and more or less settled. It's time, you both agree, for a little fun. So bring on the house-warming!

This is the sort of party that crops up now and then (most of us have been to perhaps one, but certainly not many), but is not automatically given by those who move from one place to another. Still, it is quite proper to stage such a "do." It is usually an open house, giving many guests a chance to troop over to your new address, to admire the house, congratulate you on your decorating taste, and commend you on your resourceful renovation/restoration. All of this is delightful balm for the spir-its, which may have been wilting, or even battered, through all the moving-in stress, fatigue from working on the house, dealing with the perplexing decisions you are still not sure you have resolved correctly, and the unremitting expense. After the party, you will be euphoric for days. It's worth the cost.

You must host this affair yourselves. According to etiquette expert Judith Martin, who writes the syndicated "Miss Manners" advice column, no one *ever* gives another a housewarming. So while it would have been gauche to throw yourself a bridal shower, it would be just as much of a social gaffe for a friend to give you a housewarming.

When?

The timing for this party is important and requires some thought about the condition of your home. If you have moved into a new house or condominium, or one that is at least in good shape, and virtually all you have had to do is unpack your furnishings and clothes, you can host a housewarming shortly after you are in and feel comfortable entertaining.

The older house that needs a good deal of work is trickier. Of course, no house is ever really "done," so waiting until the happy day when the last area rug is in place, and the devastatingly perfect work of art is hanging above the sofa, could put off a housewarming for years.

If some part of the unfinished house bothers you, though, try to fix it while you are planning a party. If that is not possible, entertain anyway. It is understandable that you want everything to be perfect, but in older houses, especially, some aspects of the place will never be perfect. In any event, these get-togethers are almost always informal. It is family and good friends who will attend (don't invite *everyone* you know), many or most of whom have already seen your place in its more primitive state.

There are *some* criteria that help determine the right time to hold a party, however. No housewarming should take place when there are still unopened movers' cartons littering the foyer, or when there is not enough seating for guests. It could be downright folly to hold a party if you are in a potentially dangerous stage of renovation, and company will have to navigate around ladders, scaffolds, and torn-up floors. You want to entertain, not invite a lawsuit from an injured friend.

There can be rooms still in an unfinished stage, but the overall effect does have to be welcoming and comfortable, at least in the living area. Guests should not feel they will be handed a paintbrush after they finish their mimosa.

There is no absolute cutoff date beyond which you should *not* hold a housewarming. If everyone knows you have been struggling with your nearly falling-down handyman's special, or they know that Steve is building a sunroom and you both want guests to see it finished, they will probably accept as natural a housewarming a year after you began calling that dwelling "home." In contrast, a housewarming party given one year after moving into a brand-new four-room condominium could well invite raised eyebrows.

Guests Bearing Gifts

The principal reason for being careful with the "when" of a housewarming is that almost everyone who comes will bring a present, usually something for the home. If the timing of the invitation doesn't seem quite right, it will make you both seem to be, to put it crassly, scavenging for gifts.

Housewarming gifts are not likely to be as elaborate as some shower presents were. Some folks may bring food as a gift, especially sweets. Presents should be accepted quietly, in part because you will probably be busy greeting other guests, but also because some may not bring a present, and you do not want to embarrass them. If you like, you can open a friend's gift

in the kitchen or out on the patio, but with no big show, please. Keep your expectations down, your thank-yous (notes to follow are a must) for presents effusive, and that whole aspect of the party not the center of attention.

Getting Down to Specifics

Sheila Zerrenner, who runs a Fort Lee, N.J., party and corporate planning concern called Event Makers, notes: "Young people often can't afford to hire out cleaning, or outside party planners, so you may have to do it all yourselves. That means being organized, even keeping notes, so that you can get as much work as possible out of the way by the day of the party, and can enjoy yourselves. You don't want guests to feel they have to *help* you."

There is no need to head for your nearest Party Palace Emporium to shop for this event. Jeanne Lynn of Special Occasions by Jeanne, a Los Angeles party planning service, suggests, "You don't want a lot of decorating, you want people to enjoy the house, so don't bother with balloons or covering up the home in any other way. If there is an outdoor area, it's perfectly all right to hold the party there, maybe in the yard."

Having a party in a condominium complex's clubhouse or community center is another matter. Since most housewarmings are open houses, you should have no problem entertaining in that style at home, even if your condo unit is small. If the get-together is held in some other part of the complex, it loses, obviously, the charm of a house "warming."

Can you mix your family, including your eighty-one-year-old grandmother, with your friends, who include Crazy Cal, the performance artist? Good question. The generations might not blend too well at a sit-down dinner, but all can get along fine at an afternoon open house. If you prefer, and if you can afford two parties, hold one for the family and the other for friends.

Jeanne Lynn notes that one popular housewarming style is a brunch served at 10:30 or 11:00 a.m., usually on a Sunday. A menu she suggests:

> *Champagne or mimosa cocktails*
> *Fruit salad*
> *Assorted bagels with a variety of toppings,*
> *such as cream cheese, lox and raw onion,*
> *tuna salad, seafood salad, and jellies*
> *and marmalade*
> *Scrambled eggs and chives*
> *Coffee and tea*
> *Cookies and miniature cheesecakes*

Do you prefer a late-afternoon open house? Sheila Zerrenner offers this menu:

> *White wine, sparkling cider*
> *Cold poached salmon with sesame*
> *cucumbers*
> *Crabacado—fresh lump crab meat mixed*
> *with leeks and red peppers, mounded in a*
> *ripe avocado, served with a dill sauce*
> *Swedish meatballs*
> *Lemon chicken with mushrooms and*
> *artichokes*
> *(Choose two of the above four dishes)*
> *Green and white bean vinaigrette*
> *Tomato, fresh basil, and fresh mozzarella*
> *with olive oil, garlic, and a splash of bal-*
> *samic vinegar*
> *Mixed green salad with three dressings*
> *Home-made-type (whole-grain) breads and*
> *rolls*
> *Coffee and tea*
> *Chocolate mousse, fresh fruit*

What you serve and how many people you invite will probably depend on your budget. A brunch for twelve is, of course, going to carry a smaller price tag than an open house for fifty. Since guests are likely to bring gifts, and since you want to be superb hosts in any event, you will want to make sure there is plenty to eat and drink. So don't skimp. A smaller number entertained sumptuously is better than a full house being offered only chips and dip.

A THEME?

You do not need to focus on anything specific for a housewarming, since that in itself is a theme for a party. But if a clever secondary angle comes to mind, go with it. Miss Manners, in her book *Miss Manners' Guide to Excruciatingly Correct Behavior*, mentions that the owners of one house gave a "housecooling," because a famous sex scandal had taken place there, and the house, the owners felt, was hot enough already!

One couple came up with a unique idea for their Sunday-evening open house. Their East Coast city condominium is in a restored building that was painted a cream color and given, for reasons known only to the developer, the name Santa Fe. The city is more than a thousand miles, both in distance and style, from the Southwest, but no matter. The couple's invitations, done nicely on their home computer, read: "Come to a party in Santa Fe." The hostess made her own four-alarm chili, but had a few other dishes catered from a local Mexican restaurant. The couple's essentially brown, white, and wine-colored living room lent itself well to a temporary infusion of paper flowers (complementing the decor, but not overwhelming it, as balloons would have done). He wore ordinary jeans and a cotton shirt, but she was dressed in what could generously be called a Mexican blouse, with a floor-length denim skirt and lots of jewelry. It was a theme party, certainly, but one that did not carry an idea from cleverness into cuteness.

A suburban couple who were set to entertain in *their* home, which was still in a state of disrepair, planned to wear striped overalls and paint caps to play up the idea of a work in progress. As party plans moved forward, however, they wisely decided that that garb might make their company uncomfortable. Guests might feel they were keeping the new homeowners from work, or they might think they were expected to pitch in to work on the task at hand. The hosts chucked that subtheme and played the evening straight.

A TOAST

In informal gatherings, anyone can propose a toast to Kim and Jerry and to much happiness in their new home. At more formal get-togethers, the host offers the toast. Jerry might stand at some point and thank the friends who have been good enough to come to his and Kim's new home and share this pleasant (delightful, terrific, long-awaited) evening with them. A toast to friends!

A THANK-YOU

Dropping a note to everyone who brought that "little something" to your party is in order. That could be a few words along the lines of "Dear Kate—We were so happy you both could be with us last evening. Thanks very much for the dish towels, which have already been put to good use (Ken dries!). Hope we'll see you again soon. Best, . . . Angie." (All those wedding thank-yous should make these a snap!)

It was the best, wasn't it? The glow from a really great party can last for days, to be followed by years of happy memories of your first housewarming.